THE SERAPHINA PARRISH TRILOGY

PROTECTING TRUTH

MICHELLE WARREN

Editing by Pam Berehulke
Bulletproofing | http://bulletproofing.blogspot.com
mail to: bulletproofing@live.com

Cover and book design by Michelle Preast

Thanks to my Dad,
who bought me my first telescope,
who woke me up in the middle of the night
for meteor showers, who watched Star Trek and
B.S.G. with me, and who opened my eyes and
mind to science and fantasy.

CONTENTS

"*If you want to know where your heart is,
look where your mind wanders.*"

UNKNOWN

№ 1

1

A FIGHT

I CAN'T IMAGINE AN OPPONENT LARGER THAN the one before me. His raging eyes, a tornado of blood, make our planned meeting all the more unsettling.

Clenching my arnis fighting sticks, I take a single calculated step to my left. He mirrors my action but certainly not to keep an even distance. His very existence, his purpose in life, is to fight. Mine is not.

I move slowly, crouching for balance, waiting for him to attack.

"What are you waiting for, pig?" I taunt him and laugh. The overgrown man does look like a pig; the gnarled pink flesh of his face is littered with sprigs of wiry red hair. He spits on the floor at the insult and drops a menacing grunt from his exaggerated underbite.

Although name-calling will not win points in the end, it's part of the act. I need to appear worthy of this fight, capable of winning.

My leather-clad opponent twirls both wooden sticks around his head, spinning them like helicopter blades. They whip around his back and then circle his shoulders three times, blurring with deadly speed.

"Show-off," I murmur, annoyed that I have so much more to learn.

By now, I'm positive he's sensed my fear and inexperience. I transmit it through the awkwardness with which I hold my weapon, and the nervous perspiration that drips from my neck. Inside, I wrestle my lungs for control over fits of uneven breathing, while replaying the instructions from my teacher in my head. "Sera, hide your fear behind a facade of courage," Ms. Swift, my Defense Arts instructor, would say. That would come easily to me for most things, but not for violence.

The revolting man-pig tosses each stick like a baton. They spin at turbo speed, whirling fans in the air, and land in his clenched, sausage-shaped fingers. He grins. A laugh gargles in the back of his throat.

Intuition urges me to end his games and finally attack. This match needs to be over, no matter the outcome. I inhale one last anxious breath, then, with the focus of a raging bull, I throw my petite body at his disturbingly large frame. With cunning instinct, he steps out of the way. I whip my stick, striking a horizontal blow to his head, making contact with his pointed ear. In response, his stick circles and cracks my wrist and retracts for a second nauseating blow. Each shocks my system, fueling a deep and angry fire. A scream erupts from my lips, and I roll forward and jab the blunt end of one stick into his stomach. He arches back, recoiling.

We circle each other. Tension builds, then explodes as we simultaneously attack. Our sticks clack together again and again. High backhand. Vertical blow. Whip. Snap. Inward strike. He leans in, using his Goliath strength to muscle me across the room. I lose my balance, stumbling to the floor. The moment I regain my footing, he smacks my shoulder. The hit sends me flying across the room, slamming into the mirror-covered walls. Glass cracks, shattering. Shards crash to the floor. A splintering pain shoots across my back, and I wheeze.

The creature attacks me, wrenching his sticks in alternating diagonal blows to my head. I block him, leaving myself just enough time to regain my composure. I'm standing, and we're off again. Sticks cracking, we dance across the room in a deadly fight. The sound reverberates off the mirrored walls. I want to ignore the distracting reflections created, but how can I with a behemoth man-pig, multiplied a thousand times over in the corner of my eyes? Yes, I can run away, wander into another time in history easily enough, but that's not the plan. I need to win this match.

The beast strikes my side. I return a blast to his head. That area seems to be his weakness. He drops one stick and grabs his forehead with his hoofed fingers. I strike again, a sickening crack to the back of his knees. His legs unhinge and collapse. His bulking mass falls to the floor with a thud, but he isn't done. Not yet. That would be too easy. Resting on the ground, he swipes his stick at my kneecaps. I leap over it and again when his pole swings back before he rolls to stand. With all my strength, I flip my body over his head. Landing firm, I spin to face his back.

The man-pig falters, unable to pivot quickly enough to defend himself before I raise both sticks and slice the wood through his head. The weapons cut through his skull like lasers, although in reality there are none.

He groans once more, but this time from defeat. Each half of his now divided body wisps away into the air, rolling away in bright blue electrified dust sparkles. The dissipating energy of the hologram causes my hair to stand on end as it passes. It's amazing to see something so monstrous release into something so beautiful.

"Ten minutes." A pocket watch clicks off. "You're getting much better."

I look up.

Professor Raunnebaum studies me from the classroom door, seemingly pleased with my victory.

"Not good enough." I wipe the sweat from my brow and collapse on the floor, exhausted. Both sticks roll out of my hands, far from arm's reach. There's a wound on my back from the smashed mirror, but I ignore the dull sting.

"Only ten minutes?" I ask, hyperventilating. "Felt like forever."

"Yes, but what does it matter? Improvement is improvement."

He wants me to be happy with my weeks of disciplined work, but I'm not. "Maybe we should make the lessons more difficult?" I ask. My chest heaves in and out.

"You're pushing yourself too hard, Sera. Besides, you've practically mastered every defense hologram we've created for you to fight. Turner will have to invent new characters and fighting routines to meet your evolved abilities."

"Then do it," I snap. I glance over at him just as he raises his bushy black eyebrows and crosses his arms. I know he doesn't like it when I'm bossy.

"Tell Turner the more knowledgeable and scarier the hologram, the better," I huff.

"Where's the confidence, child? Ms. Swift will be most pleased with your enhanced abilities when she returns for fall semester. Your skill level is quite good, probably much better than any Wanderer in your junior class. And possibly much better than your own Protector," he says with condemnation.

I sit up on my elbows and look at him. "It'll never be good enough." My breathing finally calms, and I force air through my nose.

"Why are you pushing yourself so hard? I've never seen a paralleled determination in another. Not even one whose position merited such rigorous training." He examines me.

I glance away, my body instinctively withdrawing from answering his question. I find my reflection in the nearest mirror and lean forward to wipe blood from my forehead, pretending I haven't heard him. The professor knows I will not answer. He's asked about my fighting obsession a million times before. I push a dark-brown flyaway behind my ear and wipe the smeared mascara from underneath my eyes.

"It feels so—unnatural—fighting," I say out loud but more to myself. I ponder the issue. "I'm performing the moves, but I'm not connected." *Hmph.* "I think more practice will help." The professor shakes his mop of erratic black hair. Every strand moves except for one pure white streak, which starts at his hairline and points off toward the ceiling. "Yes, well, don't be too hard on yourself. You're a Wanderer, after all, not a Protector." He waves his finger. Professor Raunnebaum likes to remind me of this point often as though it's an unchangeable weakness.

Unlike my team members, my job as Wanderer is to open the time travel portal, not to protect, like Bishop, and not to see a relic's life path, its entire history, like Sam.

"Does Bishop know what you've been up to?" he asks. I suspect he already knows the answer.

I sit up completely, dropping my hands on my knees. "He does," I hesitate, "but—"

"He doesn't know how much you've improved, then?" He finishes my sentence. His black eyes flicker knowingly, reading the conflict on my face. My gaze falls to the floor.

Bishop's been put in this world to protect me. As his Wanderer, my safety is his job, his life's goal. My new determination to become a better fighter means I might render Bishop useless.

True, Bishop knows a little about my training. He says he understands my need to feel in control and less like a "damsel in distress." How can he tell me *not* to become a more skilled fighter? As my Protector, his sole goal is my safety, and as my boyfriend, he happily gives me whatever I want, whether it's of a serious or a childlike nature. He's utterly selfless when it comes to my needs. Unfortunately, I seem to be the opposite, at least on this one particular point.

I throw myself onto the rubberized floor, arms and legs extended, and sigh with exaggeration.

"Don't worry, I won't tell him. I don't concern myself with teenage drama. However, there are two things you should consider, Sera. Your new zeal for fighting means interfering with the delicate balance of your three-person team. Bishop instinctively needs to protect you. If he can't or doesn't have to, it will affect his ego on a subconscious level. And second, you should come to an understanding with Turner, before he spills your training secrets to his brother." The professor chuckles. "Both might create some serious problems for you."

"Yeah, I guess you're right about that." My brow furrows.

"I'll attempt to bribe Turner later."

That's a conflict I definitely need to avoid. Bishop knowing the extent of my abilities would be inherently hurtful, yes, but his brother, Turner, knowing something about me that Bishop doesn't, might create a larger, unwanted issue. The tension between them is something I can't comprehend. Bishop only explained their dislike for each other as "sibling rivalry" and refused to say any more.

I think back to the first time I saw Turner, several months ago, the night of my first date with Bishop.

•

After returning from Paris, Bishop and I ambled, hands entwined, to our dorm apartment. We stopped at the front door and faced each other. As soon as our eyes met, he closed the distance between us in one determined motion, melding our bodies together. He placed his full, warm lips over mine, kissing me with a sweet and controlled intensity. His cupped hands caressed my cheeks, and I wrapped my arms around his waist.

The intimate moment was short. I jumped, startled when someone nearby cleared his throat. Bishop and I turned to see a boy standing down the hall, leaning against a wall. The shadows of the hallway swallowed his body, hiding his features. A nearby flickering lamp only revealed the golden contours of his face and shoulder.

"Brother," the boy said sternly and nodded at Bishop. He crossed his arms and took a confident step forward.

"Turner." Bishop stiffened and nodded.

Animosity thickened the air. Immediately, though I'd never met Bishop's fraternal twin, Turner, I wanted to escape and leave them to talk.

"Sera." Bishop turned to me. "I'll see you tomorrow, okay?" He kissed me on the forehead and opened the apartment door. He guided me in, pressing his palm into my back, shuffling me away. I looked over my shoulder, catching a glimpse of Turner. Our eyes met as he walked into the light. An inquisitive expression crossed his face, and then he grinned in such a way that forced my heart to skip a beat.

"Wait, um, okay. Night," I said confused, looking between the two.

The door shut tight, severing me from their tension. Muffled noises of an intense conversation trickled through the door. What they discussed, I couldn't make out. But soon the tones turned irate, voices raised. Someone was thrown against the door with a violent smash. They'd broken into a fight.

I rushed and swung the door open, but to my shock, the two were gone and the halls were empty.

"Bishop," I called, leaning out. My voice echoed, but no one answered.

"Bishop?" I stepped from the apartment, scanning the hallways, worried.

"I'm here." Bishop crept from the darkness, his face red. I detected a slight limp in his step and ran to him.

"What happened? Are you okay?" I eyed his leg and reached for it. "I heard you two arguing. You said you didn't get along, but…"

"It's nothing, truly. Just a normal brotherly scrap," he interrupted, and wrapped his good arm around my back to guide me inside.

•

That was months ago. At Bishop's urging, I'd let it go. But I had no idea how far the "brotherly scrap" stretched. On normal occasions they avoid each other, which seems to keep the atmosphere fairly peaceful. In fact, even after that night, weeks passed before I was properly introduced to Turner. After that, he showed up everywhere. He kept his distance, often smiling and waving from afar, but it was enough to send Bishop into hysterics. I still don't understand why.

If I continue my training in this manner, with Turner's involvement in the programming of the touchable defense holograms for my practices, their personalities will have reason to collide this coming semester. There's no way to avoid it, unless I keep my extracurricular training a secret from Bishop.

The professor takes out his pocket watch and glances at its face. "I've got to run, Sera. Turn out the lights when you're finished."

"You can turn them off now." I sigh. I don't have the energy to move from the floor.

The professor flips the switch, leaving the room pitch black, and disappears. He moves so quickly, I sometimes wonder if he's a hologram. But his speed is merely a skill developed over time, one reserved for a Protector.

I shift my body across the floor, wincing at the pain, until I've repositioned myself under an air vent to cool my over-heated body.

The quiet and darkness allow me time to meditate, to collect my thoughts, which of course are with Bishop. They always are now that he's gone home to London for summer vacation. I miss him dearly—my perfect, gorgeous Protector and boyfriend.

I groan and roll over, letting my face muscles relax on the rubberized surface. Cool air dries my drenched back. I'm a complete mess in so many ways. I exhale with exhaustion.

If Bishop knew how hard I'd been working on defense, how far I've come, I think it would not only upset him, but perhaps his quiet, sensitive ways would mislead him to be-lieve that I don't need him. Or more absurdly, that I don't want him. And if possibly hurting him isn't bad enough, my actions might tip him off to my ultimate plan: to go back in time and save my mother from the Underground—to finally finish what I started.

This time would be different, of course, because now I know my mom isn't dead. All my life I'd believed she died in a car accident because that's what my family believes. But last semester I saw her for myself, during a disastrous meet-ing with Cece, the head of the Underground—enemies of the Society of Wanderers. At the time, I was so naive that I walked Bishop and myself into a trap, a trap arranged by our backstabbing classmates Perpetua, Stu, and Jessica. In the end, Bishop and I barely escaped from the Underground with our lives.

So when I go back to face Cece and find my mom, I'll do it alone, without Bishop. I need to protect him from the truth and never allow Cece to hurt him or anyone else I care for, ever again.

A creeping sound breaks my concentration.

Still on edge from thinking about the Underground, I sit up and glance around.

"Who's there?"

No

2

TURNER

M Y BODY TENSES, SCANNING FOR A FIGURE
creeping against the darkened mirrors. Out of the
stillness, a boy speaks.

"She rests quietly in darkness/under a perfect cloudless
sky/dreaming of Seraphim angels/with which she conspires,"
the boy recites. But whether the words are his own poetry or
someone else's, I'm not sure.

Hearing his familiar voice, raspy with a British accent, I
relax.

"Haven't you heard it's not nice to sneak up on people?"

"You seem so peaceful resting there. I dare say, it compelled me to speak in verse," he says in a playful, sophisticated tone.

"You're weird, Turner." A point I have never said out loud but have thought often.

"Quite possibly." He flicks the light switch on. I glance up from where I rest.

He leans lazily against the wall with his arms across his chest, hands resting on his shoulders, a strange pose he often takes. His dark wavy hair, a well-coordinated mess, falls into his eyes and frames his cheekbones. His physical appearance, that of a fraternal twin, is similar in beauty to Bishop's, but different, in a darker, complex manner. The intensity of his silvery slate-colored eyes always hold my gaze until they embarrass me, and I'm forced to look away, face red and burning with heat.

"I hate it when you stare at me like that," I say, to make him feel as guilty as I do.

"I'm not sure what you mean, Seraphina." He strolls forward with dramatic confidence.

"I wish you wouldn't call me that."

"Why?"

"Just don't. Okay?" The longer, formal version of my name feels of a more intimate nature, one that I exclusively reserve for Bishop.

"As you wish, my lady." He bows as though rolling an imaginary feather cap from his head, and then he holds out his palm. A small package sits inside his curled fingers.

"For you," he says.

"What's this?" I grab the box.

"Don't know. Ms. Midgenet asked me to deliver it." He unsnaps the cuffs of his long-sleeve shirt and then rolls them up to his elbows while I inspect the package.

I turn the brown paper-covered box around in my hand and squint at the return address. One glance leaves me electrified. I hadn't expected the delivery to arrive so quickly. I repress a smile, remembering Turner always watches me closely. Too closely. I clear my throat.

"Thanks," I say, pulling myself from the floor.

"Aren't you going to open it?" He cocks his head, trying to decipher the look on my face.

"Later." I shrug. I dip the box behind my back and hope the old phrase "out of sight, out of mind" holds true.

"Really?" A mischievous smile rolls across his lips. "I think," he says, looking at the ceiling as though he's in deep contemplation, then starts to pace with a finger at his lips. He stops and turns to face me. "No. We should open it now!" He charges, swipes the tiny box from my hands, and vanishes, running in the opposite direction, out the door of the training room.

Without thinking, I chase after him. His speed, a blur in time, is unmatched by any other student Protector. And I, of course, am merely a Wanderer, not the team member normally known for speed.

When I reach the door, he's already rounded the corner

at the opposite end of the hallway, two hundred feet away, headed through Olde Town, the ancient underground city below Washington Square Academy for Wanderers.

Desperation forces me forward. The last thing I want is for him to open the package. But I know that, being Turner, he will. After so many of his childish pranks, I'm convinced the boy walks this earth to aggravate me.

Several hundred stairs later, I find him, as expected, in the laboratory. Chalkboards with scientific diagrams, inventions, and complex contraptions cram the claustrophobic space. Each seems to be of another, earlier century, although what they do is beyond current technology. Silver steam crawls through at regular intervals. I suspect the fog has much to do with the weather machine Professor Raunnebaum designed to keep Olde Town a perfect, year round, seventy-two degrees.

I maneuver around several intricate machines with large cranks, bronze pipes, and multicolored gauges. If I weren't so obsessed with defending myself from possible meetings with the Underground and finding my mom, I might visit this room more often to investigate all the intriguing inventions. And maybe, I amend, if the annoying Turner weren't here all the time, working as the professor's assistant.

Thick smoke clears just enough to notice the small ripped pieces of brown paper at my feet. Little shreds, like pieces of bread, wind their way through the room on the floor, making a trail especially designed for me to follow. The paper trail can only mean one thing. Turner's opened my package.

I grind to a stop. Angry heat rushes to my face. My hands clench at my sides, and I consider my options. It's important to keep my feelings under wraps. I cannot, under any circumstances, allow him to know the importance of the package's contents.

Taking deep breaths, I control my temper. My blood pressure drops, and I relax my shoulders. When I regain my composure, I walk on to find him.

Turner appears out of a puff of hazy smoke. He smiles, pleased with himself. His sculpted arms hang lazily, flung over the back of a mohair-covered couch. He tilts his head back, relaxing his neck, and stares at the wood-beamed ceiling.

"Seraphina, you're so incredibly slow," he says in an exasperated drawl.

"Please don't call me that." I frown.

He lifts his head and careless black locks of hair fall forward, partially covering his face. Dazzling eyes land intently on mine, again. Always staring. Turner's eyes always seem to search mine in that sultry manner. What is he looking for?

I look away from his annoyingly handsome face. My gaze falls on the box. It rests on an overstuffed ottoman before him. He's unwrapped the outer paper. From here, it's unclear if he's opened the box to see what's inside.

"Don't you want to open it?" He smirks.

I exhale, attempting to act unfazed, but don't answer.

"Don't worry, you can take it now. I've had my fun," he says seriously, but I'm not sure if he's teasing, still playing games.

I raise my eyebrows and place my hands on my hips, remaining silent.

"Really, take it. It's yours, after all."

My eyes never leave his, no matter how uncomfortable they make me feel. He enjoys toying with me, so I'm not positive if he will jump up, grab the box, and disappear again.

I inch toward the ottoman. When my shins butt against the edge, I bend down and quickly scoop up the package. My fingers curl around its edges and I relax, knowing it's in my possession again.

"See, I told you."

"Whatever, Turner. Really, you're a pain, you know?"

"I try." He grins. "Seriously, why don't you open it?"

"Later!" Completely agitated, I turn to walk away.

"Professor Raunnebaum mentioned that you needed to discuss something with me," he calls out.

Right. I forgot. I swing around. "Yeah—that. I need a few more defense holograms."

"Already? You've mastered all thirty-six?"

"Yeah." I cough, waving away a silver plume of smoke.

"I'm impressed." He's thoughtful for a moment. "Although, it seems unnecessary to program more defense routines when Bishop returns tomorrow, and your Defense Arts classes will start soon."

"About that—"

"Yes?" He says the word with cautious curiosity.

I pace, looking at the floor. "I was hoping—I—we—could keep my summer defense training off the record? I mean..." I exhale, looking for the proper words, ones that seem less alarming. "Of course, Bishop knows I've been practicing, but I really don't want him or anyone to know how intently I've been working." I hesitate and stop to face him. "Like a surprise," I lie with a tight smile.

He sits in attention, folding his hands on his legs and leans into the conversation. "Really?"

"Yes." I begin to pace again. "In fact, I want to continue the lessons, shall we say—on the side. Quietly, of course."

"Hmm." He sinks into the maroon couch, regarding me with suspicion.

Clocks tick, machines crank, and another plume of smoke rolls through the room. But he doesn't answer. He only looks at his fingernails, acting preoccupied and bored.

"Well?" I put my hand on my hip.

"Well—you know how I would love to keep the secret for you, but..." He waves his hand with a dismissive flip.

"But—what?" Nerves jolt my body. I cross my arms, trying to control myself. Even telling Turner as little as this without an agreement could create real tension between him and Bishop. I can imagine Turner now, acting like a child, taunting Bishop with the secrets he knows. I roll my eyes, pushing the thought out of my head.

"You're putting me in quite a predicament," Turner finally

responds.

"Do tell, Turner." I lean on a nearby machine.

"Well, if Bishop were to ever find out, it would be my extremely handsome head on a platter."

"That's the whole idea. He can't find out," I force through gritted teeth.

"Well then, I'm afraid, I won't be able to help you. I'm endeavoring to be a better brother."

"Ha!" I say reflexively, but when I inspect him closer, he isn't smiling. "Are you serious?"

"Quite." He nods.

"Of all the times he has to choose to be a good brother," I snarl under my breath, and turn to stomp away.

"That is, of course, unless you want to tell me what you're doing with this lovely relic you ordered from Rome?"

№ 3

A CHALLENGE

I STOP IN MY TRACKS WHEN HE SAYS THE words and realize the box in my hand is empty. My anger multiplies a thousandfold when I spin to see the new relic I just ordered from Rome, a black beaded rosary, hanging from his fingertips.

"It's a pretty little thing, Sera." He looks at me. "So where might this lovely relic be taking you in history?"

"You said you didn't open it!" I scream and throw the empty box at his face. He ducks to the side, easily evading the flying object.

"Temper, temper," he tuts, shaking his head. His provoking smirk returns. *The game continues.*

"It must be of real importance to you." He stands, then circles dangerously like I'm some kind of weak prey.

"I never said that I didn't open it. You merely assumed." He smiles. "Quite wrongly, of course. You should know better."

Instead of thinking, I just attack. I jump, reaching for the necklace, but my small frame can't compete with his height. He dangles the beads higher in the air. I find myself pawing at his body to gain some momentum. The thought of seriously injuring him crosses my mind, but he speaks before our fight escalates.

"As much as I like this attention, I think you should calm down. I'm positive we can come to an agreement."

"What's that supposed to mean?" I throw myself into a nearby chair, crossing my arms across my body, pouting. No sense in hiding my feelings now.

He sits on the arm of the sofa. "What I mean is, you have a favor you need of me—and well—I have something I'd like to ask from you. In return, of course."

"Of course!" Agitated, I look away, letting my cheek rest upon my palm. I ignore him for a few moments, letting my gaze drift around the cluttered workroom, allowing myself time to understand his personal agenda and ultimately devising how I might get my way. But there is no way, of course, because Turner is absolutely impossible.

He clears his throat. "It's not much, I promise."

"Fine." I moan, letting my head fall back. "Spill."

"Well, I'd be willing to keep your secret from everyone, including your precious Bishop, and keep you supplied with new defense holograms, *if* you tell me two little things." He smiles, knowing he has me.

"What?"

"Tell me," he stands and paces, "why are you so obsessed with mastering defense, and what are you doing with this necklace?"

"That's none of your business!" My body flings forward.

"You'll tell me." He circles the space, casting his devious eyes over his shoulder, and then he sits, relaxing back into the couch.

My eyes narrow.

"I have a feeling—a hunch really, that they might be related. What do you think of that hypothesis?"

"You're way off!" I fume. But really, he isn't. His guess is spot-on. *Am I really that easy to read? If so, I'll never be able to hide my plan, especially from Bishop. He knows me better than anyone.*

I look over at Turner, this time intensifying my evil eye. I wish I had laser eyes for a superpower rather than time travel, so I could burn the word "turd" onto his forehead. But when he flashes those sultry eyes again, I lift myself out of the chair and walk away without saying another word. I'm too annoyed.

There's no way I'm becoming indebted to him. That would be about as smart as entering into an agreement with the Devil. *I'll get my rosary necklace back——somehow.*

"Seraphina! Really, I'm only looking after you!" he yells in amusement. I cringe, irritated further by my full name.

I wind my way through the smoke-filled laboratory, kicking the pieces of brown paper aside as they appear out of swirling clouds. Then I exit the laboratory, slamming the door on the way out.

In the hallway I pace, conflicted. *Should I return to bargain with him?* I know he won't give in until he gets his way. And *I* won't surrender until I get mine. Right now, telling him the truth, answering his questions, simply isn't an option I can entertain, because not one soul knows my plan for that necklace——to use it as a relic to go back and rescue my mom from the Underground.

The rosary relic was sent all the way from Rome, Italy, because finding a suitably aged relic in the Relic Archives had proven impossible. Anything within a year old would still be waiting to be cataloged by Argus Matchimus, the relics curator.

The small jewelry dealer I purchased the rosary from sat mere blocks away from the church in which I found my mom on the day I used the Egyptian sundial bracelet to wander from Chicago to Rome. To be sure, I don't know if I found her in "true time" by skipping (moving from one moment to the next without losing or gaining time), or if the encounter transpired sometime in recent history. Using the Egyptian sundial bracelet had made it impossible to know for sure.

When I think to the piazza in Rome that day, everyone appeared to be dressed in clothing from the current time. But the biggest clue was that Francis and Jessica were there. As Seers, they would have arrived in a normal way, not via wandering. Still, pinpointing the exact day is difficult. And I refuse to ask Sam, my Seer, even though her ability to see the events as they transpired through Bishop's eyes will allow her to make an educated guess. Sam is the only other person who knows my mother is alive. I swore her to secrecy months ago. Bringing up the experience again might alert her to my plan. I can only hope that she's forgotten. Or, to be more accurate, I hope she's filed it away in the back of her mind, as much as a Wanderer can.

I lean against the wall, angry with myself for losing the relic to Turner's games. I press my hand to my stomach, feeling sick.

Footsteps approach from behind the laboratory door. Not wanting to confront Turner until I can consider my options, I keep moving.

I mope through Olde Town, taking my time, letting the fake sun warm my skin. I collapse into a metal chair under a tree and watch the champagne-colored butterflies dance around the golden obelisk. The pillar stands several stories tall in the center of the plaza of the underground city. The top third of the obelisk sits aboveground, outside, in the court-yard of Washington Square Academy for Wanderers.

I glance around the buildings. Olde Town is completely

empty, except for a few tropical-looking birds that have made the city their permanent home. A manufactured breeze rolls through. It ruffles the bright green leaves in the tree's canopy and pushes the butterflies farther away, toward a crumbling building with Victorian details.

True, I'm not ready to face any aged Wanderer, Protector, or Seer to fight for my mom. They'd be much more powerful than I, even with all my hard work. If I'm being honest with myself, I still might be years away from the peak of my abilities, whatever they may be. So if I have to weasel the necklace away from Turner over a short time, it would be okay. This eases my mind. After more consideration, I'm mostly disturbed by Turner's games and his obvious attempt to control me. *Why can't he just leave me alone, be nice, and choose another girl to stare at with his hypnotic eyes?*

The clock on the Tower Building strikes twelve with a deep gong that vibrates my skin. This cheers me slightly, and I roll my aching body to stand. I walk through the nearest stone archway, the Lion's Gate, and cross the worn redwood bridge, leaving Olde Town.

Two metal lions stand guard on their pedestals. Their rusted gears grind and activate, creating a dull roar. I should be used to it by now. The Animates always stir when I'm near, but I quickly jump into the ornate elevator and slam the retractable gate shut, locking it into place, just in case they decide that this is the day they will finally attack. I crank the handle until the elevator ascends toward the main floor of the Academy.

A few moments later, I stand in a large vestibule off the main entrance. Mailboxes stack high, twenty feet into the air on the walls, encircling me. But these are not normal mailboxes. They're of the Animate variety. Similar to the lions in Olde Town, they and other metal statues here magically live and breathe.

When the mailboxes sense my presence, they snap to attention with a metallic whack. With the precision of a fine timepiece, wheels and cogs revolve and click, rotating the boxes from top to bottom and left to right, like the largest Rubik's Cube known to man. The Animate, solving the intricate puzzle, presents my mailbox—number 42508.

I touch my finger to the recognition thumb pad, and the mailbox lock clicks. The bronze door swings open, and I shove my hand into the dark cubicle, grabbing a wad of envelopes. Huddling the stack to my chest, I close the door and step away as the mailboxes rearrange themselves.

Leaning against a nearby column, I shuffle through the papers. I stop on a beautiful postcard. Fancy script announces, "Greetings from Taormina, Sicily." Aunt Mona returned to Italy for the summer on a painting tour.

I flip to the next piece of mail—a large golden envelope from my dad, Ray. I keep going, pretending not to care about what he's sent. I'm still angry with him for our non-summer. We'd planned to spend several weeks together, even planning a Hawaiian vacation. But not long after I returned home to Miami, work summoned him. Annoyed, I decided not to wait around. I've never been a priority in his eyes. So one week after school ended, I returned to the Academy and started a rigorous training schedule.

Finally, I flip to the envelope I hoped for—a letter from Bishop. I smile and admire the red stamp of Queen Elizabeth. Just this small item eases the annoyance of the morning's activities.

Thrilled, I dart up the main staircase and down the long marble corridor to my apartment. I shove the mail between my legs and pull out my keys to unlock the antique crystal doorknob.

"Seraphina."

I look over my shoulder to see who calls.

No. 4

LOVE LETTERS

I STEADY MY EYES, TAKING IN THE IMAGE twenty feet away.

A cloaked hologram wavers, hovering just above the shiny marble floor, where I can see its reflection mirrored.

"Seraphina." The hologram speaks again.

I snap to attention at the name, certain that Turner sent the hologram to taunt me. This is his sad attempt at sarcasm. He'll probably make all the holograms call me Seraphina from now on, just to tick me off.

"I've finished my defense lesson for the day," I command. This should shut the machine off, but it doesn't. Instead, the image steps forward.

"I said—I've already done my exercises for the day!" I yell.

"Yes, I've seen." Another voice speaks nearby, too close for comfort. I jump, dropping my mail and it scatters across the floor. A few pieces land on Terease Ivanov's black boot. She's appeared from an adjacent hallway.

"Oh—you," I say unenthusiastically and peek around her black leather-clad body to make sure the hologram got the message. Swirls of electrified dust coil, evaporating into thin air. *Good.* The last thing I want to do is tell Turner that one of his stupid hologram machines malfunctioned. *Spft.*

"Who was that?" she asks suspiciously in her Russian accent.

"Just one of Turner's inventions," I explain. "What do you want? I didn't know you were back." I lean down to collect the mail.

When I look up, she's examining me skeptically, probably considering the hologram. I hope she'll just let it go. It's not unusual for the professor and Turner to install inventions around the school.

"What?" I demand again and stand straight, giving her the defiant face I normally reserve for my dad, Ray. You could say Terease and I have an uncomfortable history.

Her eyes narrow with her usual contempt. "Meet me in my office, tomorrow afternoon at four. We have much to discuss."

Before I can turn away, her coal-black eyes engage mine. Our minds lock together, and she lights one simmering spark. The flames explode with the force of lit kerosene. Quickly the uncontrolled wildfire whips and races through my maze of thoughts and memories. I fight her psychological rampage, helplessly attempting to force her out of my head. I squeeze my hands over my temples, clench my teeth, and gag at the taste of sulfur foaming in my mouth. *Get out! Get out!* I scream inside.

She releases me.

Immediately my muscles seize into painful cramps, and I collapse to the floor on my hands and knees, panting. I look up, and Terease walks away. Her high-heeled boots click the corridor floor.

"Sounds like fun," I respond sarcastically to her meeting request.

She just laughs her sandpapery laugh. The evil sound echoes, bouncing off the cavernous halls. A sickly cape of darkness follows her, dragging along the marble floor, murals, and columns until she rounds the corner, pulling the shadows from view.

Strangely, I seem to be the one person who evades her special abilities as a Harvester. With a normal Wanderer, she can search their brains, pluck thoughts, pull memories, and extract information. But with me, she can only burn my mind. What purpose this serves, I have yet to understand. For now, I consider it a type of child abuse or an act of dominance.

Recovering on the floor, I rub my forehead. Unfortunately, the short-term results of her burn sessions are massive headaches. The long-term effect—I'm not exactly sure yet, but I'm positive it involves a butt load of lost brain cells.

I moan and roll over. With wavering enthusiasm, I gather my mail, leaving it in a pile on the floor. Turning, I jiggle the door lock, trying to pop the apartment door open from a kneeling position. When the door finally opens, I lean in and hold on to the knob steady myself, then lift my body.

The doorknob pops off in my hand, sending me crashing back to the ground. I rest for a few moments, considering my bad luck. With all the energy I have left, I lug myself into the apartment, drag a nearby chair across the room, and wedge it against the door as a temporary doorstop. It won't keep out anyone who really wants in, but I'm not expecting any visitors at the moment.

Walking through the apartment, I pick up several pairs of dirty socks, push through my bedroom door, and drop the stack of mail on my bed. My room and apartment are a colossal mess. Sam, impeccable to a fault, will die if she arrives home to this unsalvageable wreckage. She and Bishop, as my team members, are also my roommates. I promise myself to clean it up tomorrow, but first, I need to take care of myself. Immediately, I take an extra long, extra hot shower.

When I slip into my oversized robe, my muscles relax,

finally at ease. My burning headache is a dull memory. I linger by the bed, towel-drying my hair and eyeing Bishop's unopened letter. Normally, I hold off reading them for as long as possible. When I can no longer force myself to wait another minute, the rush of reading his words is all the more satisfying and exhilarating. But today, I can't wait. The ache of missing him is at a heightened peak, probably because I'm anticipating his return to Chicago tomorrow.

He made me promise not to wander to see him in London over the summer holiday, which is absolutely ridiculous. Somewhere in his Protector mind, he considers me vulnerable. After last semester, he fears Cece and the Underground will hunt me down again.

When he looked imploringly at me with those beautiful green eyes, I reluctantly promised to lock myself away in the Academy for the summer, with only his letters to remind me of him. And those letters—they're simply beautiful, romantic letters.

I collect the cream envelope and walk out of my bedroom and into the living area. I grasp the handle of Bishop's bedroom door, rotate the knob, and peek in. My brain knows the room is empty, but I always hope, wish, that Bishop will appear, leaning back in his chair with his feet anchored on his desk, reading a tattered book, just as he always had during the spring semester.

He'd smile brightly and say, "Hello, love," in that delightfully British way, his perfect, lopsided smile revealing a ghost of a dimple. The smile would reach his eyes, bending them into arcs, accentuating his thick-fringed lashes. I'd do anything to look into those sparkling green eyes right now.

I exhale when I register the empty room. Afternoon sunlight barely filters through the curtains' sheers. I meander to his bed, still unmade from my last visit, and sink down into it, relaxing into the fluff as my tiptoes barely graze the wood floor. Rocking back, I swing my legs on top of the down comforter and nestle my head into his feather pillow.

The pillow smells like him, even after all this time— weeks. His aftershave lingers, warm citrus and leather. I inhale the intoxicating aroma. My eyelids flutter. Bishop's stunning face dances behind them. If I could only hold this thought forever, I'd be in heaven.

Giving in, I break the wax seal on his envelope, slide my finger under the open corner, and tear. Instantly, I regret it. *Why don't I have the strength to wait? Why does he have this unexplainable hold over me?*

Ornate script decorates the cream page. He's been working on his penmanship, practicing calligraphy. He explained that my letters deserved to be beautiful. I smell the paper first. The ink is still tart and fresh.

My Seraphina,

All I can think of are the coming days.
When we can unite once more, promise me this:
Nourish my heart, for it has been starved.
Feed my eyes, for they are weak.
Satisfy my touch, for my hands lay quiet.
Restless. Waiting. Dreaming.
Until I fall into your sweet embrace,
Feel the ebb and tide of your chest,
Become drunk once more by your sweet breath,
Consumed, forever lost, in the wild violets of your gaze.

Restless. Waiting. Dreaming.
— Bishop

I reread the words out loud, memorizing them with my special gift of perfect recall. I want to capture these perfect, loving emotions in my thoughts forever.

My body and shoulders tighten with each reading and, in this moment, I decide I must see him. I can't wait any longer. With his beautiful letter in hand, I can wander through time, directly to him. I just have figure out how to leave the Academy without anyone catching me.

№
5

THE LAUNCH

I'VE NOT ONLY BEEN ON LOCKDOWN AT THE Academy for Bishop's sake, even though I pretend that's the case for my own sanity. The thought of someone telling me what to do always seems like a challenge for me to do the opposite.

Now that Terease is back, she'll enforce the lockdown herself. The entire staff, at least what is left for the summer, watch me like hawks. I can't even leave the Academy grounds without a chaperone. They know about my confrontation with Cece last winter and won't allow a repeat performance. Little do they realize, that's exactly what I want—eventually.

I stand in the turret of my room, staring out the bed-room door on the far side of the room. The furniture was a pain in the butt to move, but with it pushed to the side, near the walls, there's a bare stretch of running space from my bedroom all the way through the living area. Even still, there doesn't seem to be enough space to run and launch my-self into a time-traveling wormhole. I have a sneaking suspi-cion that the apartments are designed this way on purpose. The Academy doesn't want students to wander within their rooms, with no security cameras to record the event.

Gripping Bishop's letter in my hand as a relic, I run re-gardless. I have to try to wander; I have to see him. If I use his name in my mind as the keyword to unlock the time-traveling door, the relic will transport me to London, where he last touched the envelope.

"Bishop, Bishop, Bishop."

I pump my arms hard, push my legs to long strides, and hope for maximum speed. I run past the bed, out the bed-room door, past the mini kitchen and the sectional sofa. I close my eyes and pray for a miracle.

My body slams into the living room wall.

"Uggh!" I hit the floor, crushing my shoulder, knocking the wind from my chest. Above my head, the TV wobbles, unsteady. I scramble out of its path, but thankfully, it doesn't fall.

"That's not going to work," I grunt.

Annoyed, I rest, thinking of alternate locations. With no

conclusion, I pick myself up off the floor and walk around the school to scope out other possibilities—if there are any.

I begin in a place I've never ventured—the Academy's attic. The elevator's cage opens into a rough space with slanted ceilings. There's a light switch, a large cast iron bubble anchored to the wall with two buttons. I push both at the same time. A buzzing noise shoots electricity through wires in the ceiling, breathing life into the overhead bulbs with an electric pop. Orange sparks rain down from the fixtures, and the lights flicker eerily.

I glance around, searching for the blue blinking lights that accompany the video surveillance system, otherwise known as the E.Y.E.S. Happily, there are none.

In the small room, there's an oversized door. A crooked sign reads, "NO STUDENTS. ACADEMY PERSONNEL ONLY!" The words are handwritten and faded. The poster hangs, barely affixed with a tack. I rip the sign down and toss it to a nearby table. I wonder if they really think a sign will deter me. *There must be something good in there.*

I reach for the doorknob but hesitate. Even though there are no cameras, an alarm might sound. You just never know in this place.

Curiosity has the better of me at this point, and I step forward. The elevator door slams shut with a clack. I jolt at the sound and turn to see the cage dropping out of sight, droning off for another floor. I release my breath, now realizing I had been holding it all this time.

When I return my attention back to the forbidden door, it's popped open, just an inch. *No alarm.* I push the door with my fingertip. It creaks, drifting halfway open. Tipping my head in, I survey the space before committing to a full entry.

Open-caged rooms wrap confusingly, making an iron maze. Deciding I'm alone, I walk to the nearest cage, grab onto the iron bars, and rest my cheeks between them to survey the contents. Boxes, clothes, and furniture stack from the floor to the ceiling, nestled in neat, tidy, shelving compartments. The lock on the gate is old, at least a hundred years. I turn it over. A name is etched into the back. Maybe these are personal effects of teachers or something, like a storage facility, but I can't be sure.

The droning sound returns and the cage door of the elevator clacks open. Two people move about the entrance area, chatting. Worried that I'll be caught, I run, searching for a hiding spot.

"You left the door open?" one man accuses another.

"I don't know, man. Maybe. So what?"

"*So what?* If Terease saw this, we'd lose our jobs!" The man grunts with understandable annoyance. "Just watch where you're pushing this thing!"

Two men appear from behind the door, rolling a cart full of luggage. I crouch down farther.

They stop. One man takes out a clipboard and reads it. "Each of these goes into a different locker. Looks like they go back here."

I imagine the man pointing in the direction I'm hiding because that seems to be the direction they're moving. As the sound closes in, I crawl on my hands and knees through the maze. Somewhere in the middle, I find a new spot. Peeking through the piles of boxes and assorted crap, I barely see them.

The man in charge takes out a clanking set of keys and unlocks several gates. He reads out numbers from the clipboard as the second man finds the correlating bag, lugs it into the proper cage, and shoves it neatly into a compartment. They repeat this about ten times before they finally leave, locking the cages and finally the main door behind them.

"Great!" Locked in. Now I really have to find a way out.

I drag myself from the floor and walk the maze, looking for the blue blinking lights of the E.Y.E.S. When I'm positive there are none, I walk the room again, seeking a long stretch of space that will allow me to run and launch myself into time, hopefully to be with Bishop.

From my view, there's one possible exit. The long walkway against the south wall is mostly clear and definitely long enough to send me to London. There's just the matter of moving the two oversized objects that seem very strategically placed on its path. The smaller item I manage to move with the full weight of my body leaning against it. The distance, only a few inches, makes all the difference in the world. The second, a cast iron safe the size of a dishwasher, won't budge. On its own it weighs a ton, not including whatever resides inside.

I stand on one side of the long stretch, considering the possibilities. If I run from this direction, the safe sits at the farthest point in my run. I might be able to jump on top and launch myself into time at the last second. *Maybe.* If I don't succeed, it will really hurt.

At the far end of the room, I take my position and roll my neck, jiggle my arms and legs, then crouch into a starting stance. I remove Bishop's letter and grasp it in my hand.

"Bishop." I say his name out loud as though he's my religion, completely certain that my faith will take me to him.

"Bishop." I say it again, imagining every alluring part of him.

"Bishop." I inhale, imagining his sublime scent encompassing my body.

I clench the letter and say his name again, forgetting everything else.

"Bishop." His name becomes the keyword in my mind that will send me to him.

I open my eyes, certain that I see him at the end of my path. I run toward the vision, arms pumping and legs stretched, running like lightning. Cages fly past, filled with forgotten boxes. I launch my body onto the large safe, toes grabbing, projecting me off the iron box, my arms reaching toward the sky.

"Bishop."

№ 6

LONDON

ATTIC DUST EXPLODES. WOOD FLOORS CRACK, splitting into jagged shards. Metal fencing groans and bends in half. The room rolls over on itself with the force of a crashing ocean wave. The resulting current sends luggage and lost belongings flying through the air. I barely escape a gate threatening to stab my leg before a glittering wormhole swallows me whole. I bounce twice off the rubber-like walls traveling to the location where Bishop last interacted with my relic—his love letter.

A blinding light appears and spits me out of the wormhole, skidding across a sidewalk. In the chaos, I dodge several pedestrians before falling to the ground. Miniscule rocks and dirt impale my knees and hands, and pricks of blood ooze from my rash-burned skin. An older man stops to help me up. I smile, thanking him, and brush my palms on my skirt, happy that the fabric camouflages blood within its red pattern. Large cherry-colored bruises dot my legs, making me look like a schoolchild that's fallen while playing in a park. But I'm not in a park, and I'm not even at Washington Square Academy anymore. I'm in London, the day Bishop sent this letter.

He must be close.

I tuck the letter into my jacket pocket and lift on tippy-toes to scan the noisy city street. A red postal box stands nearby. I run and jump on it, grabbing onto the decorative finial at the top in an effort to lift my short frame above the crowds. Bishop must have just dropped the letter here, in this box. He's nearby—somewhere.

The roads, the traffic, the movement of the people all point in a single direction, maybe toward an underground rail station. The sun hides behind silvery clouds, low in the sky. It's rush hour. These commuters are heading home or to the nearest pub for the evening.

I jump off the postal box and run in the direction of the commuters, hoping that Bishop will be among them. I visually sweep the crowd for his tousled, chocolate-colored hair.

"Bishop!" I weave through people, calling his name.

The crowd tightens, blocking my view, and I search for a

new way to elevate myself. A black clock tower stands ahead. I run to it and hoist my body upon the mini version of Big Ben.

"Bishop!" I scream, entwining my fingers into an ornate iron design.

"Bishop!"

A face finally turns in response, acknowledging the name, but it isn't Bishop. The girl's waves of dark hair wind around her face, only revealing her blue-violet eyes.

My mouth drops open in shock.

She is *me*.

I lock eyes with the girl, looking for her reaction. Is she surprised to see me? Her eyes are red-rimmed and teary, but somehow she's not shocked that I'm sharing the same space. Unconcerned, she merely turns and moves with the direction of the crowd.

Jumping down, I follow at a safe distance. Whatever that might be; I'm not sure. *Am I dangerous to myself? Stupid to think so.* Obviously she's from the future, visiting the past. But how far ahead has she traveled from?

The Society of Wanderers frowns upon interacting with yourself. Maybe that's why she ignores me and walks away, but I follow, regardless. If I really have to, I can go to Bishop's home later since I have his address memorized. This will be a short detour, I promise myself. What can it hurt?

The girl walks determined as though on a mission, past the iron clock, through the median, and across the road. She confidently dodges several black taxis along her route.

I'm not quite as brave. I stand on the edge of the road; wind blows my hair as autos whiz past. Through wispy strands, I see her run farther in clothes I don't recognize, past rows of idle red double-decker buses. She ducks into an elaborate window-covered building. Large black letters on its oversized awning read LONDON VICTORIA STATION.

When the traffic breaks, I dart across the walkway with several other determined commuters. The girl, my mirror image, walks far ahead of me, so I run.

By the time I reach the doors to the train station, the crowd pushes in on itself, funneling into the inadequate opening of the facade. I squeeze through, clearing the mob, and find the girl lingering on the other side. When she sees me, she darts away. Maybe she's meeting someone? Bishop?

The train station's ceiling soars high above, with glass walls and steel latticework. A mash of people crowd around, chatting in many different languages. The muffled sound of the overhead speaker echoes, announcing train delays and de-tours. In the commotion, I almost miss the girl, disappearing into a dark tunnel. I follow at a comfortable distance. She stops to buy a ticket at a fare machine and I mirror her action. Thank goodness I have my credit card. How will I explain a charge in London to Ray?

Trailing behind, I follow her down a set of stairs, an esca-lator, and into the underground rail station. On the platform, a streamlined train screams to a halt. The girl enters one side of the train car, I on the other. From here, I can only see her hair. She's hidden behind a woman reading a book.

Where's she going?

Commuters cram uncomfortably into every available nook and cranny. The train speeds forward for several minutes, making silent bobbleheads out of every person. The train stops twice, once at St. James Park and again at Westminster, but the girl stays put. The conductor announces the next stop as Embankment, and she turns to face the door.

The train stops and the door slides open. Commuters push out as many more push in. I squeeze through them and follow the girl as she races along the platform to the exit, up the stairs and escalators, and into the open air. When I arrive aboveground, the scent of the nearby river hits me.

I scan for the girl again and easily find her heading north on the river's embankment. She walks slower now, with a cell phone scrunched between her ear and shoulder. *When will I get a new cell phone?*

I hang back, trying not to interact, just watching. I lose sight of her for a few moments, but when I walk past a grouping of trees, something familiar comes into view. The grand obelisk stands sixty feet high, pointing skyward—Cleopatra's Needle. I've been here before with my team, on my way to find my mom with the Egyptian bracelet last semester.

The girl sits at the base of the obelisk, staring at something in her hand. It's small and shiny. She glances in my direction but stares straight past me. Tears muddled with mascara weave rivers of black ink over her rosy cheeks. Her head falls heavy into her shivering hands.

Instantly my heart aches. Even though I have no idea why she's crying, I run in her direction, ready to console her. I reach my arm out, ready to call her name.

"Sera!"

But when I hear the name out loud, it isn't my voice. Rotating, I see Bishop. He stands in the path behind me, staring with a furious and confused expression.

"Bishop?"

I turn to the girl, but she's gone.

"Sera? What are you doing here?"

I run to him, ignoring his question, and throw my arms around his waist, melting into the curve of his body. His delicious warmth radiates around me. His angry tension releases, and he finally hugs me back.

I look up; he cups my cheeks within his hands and leans down to kiss me. Lightly at first and more determined, maybe, as he realizes I'm really here.

"Sorry," I say.

"Don't ever be sorry for a kiss," he says in his velvety British accent.

"Are you mad at me for breaking my promise?"

"Terribly, I afraid." He laughs his perfect laugh and kisses my forehead. His long arms seem to wrap around my waist twice, making me feel secure.

"How did you know where to find me?"

"When I spoke to you on the phone a few moments ago, you said you were at Cleopatra's Needle. And here you are."

"Hmph." My *other me*, the one chatting on the cell phone, must have called him.

"Are you still mad?"

"At first, when you called. But then…"

"Then what?"

"I saw you." He smiles brighter, if that's even possible. A dimple punctuates his cheek, and he holds me skintight to his side and squeezes.

"I missed you so much."

"Me too."

I don't mention the other me. Apparently, Bishop didn't notice her. I gaze into his sparkling green eyes, hidden behind a fringe of thick lashes. The only thing I want to worry about is the person beside me—my Protector.

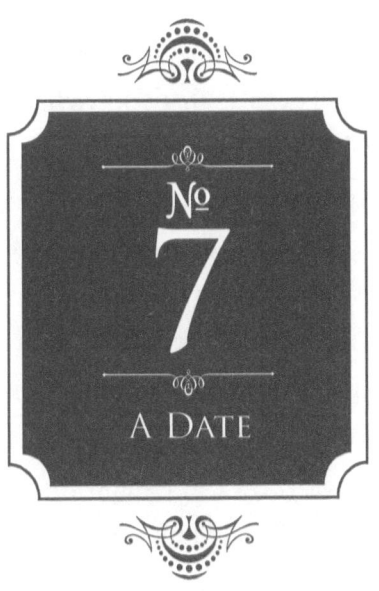

No
7

A DATE

B ISHOP AND I SETTLE ON A BENCH ALONG THE
riverbank. Two ornate cast iron camels hold worn pieces
of wood that serve as the seat.

Bishop's eyes move back and forth as he scans the prom-
enade. He's always looking for danger.

"So, how did you get here?"

"Your letter." I remove the crumpled envelope from my
pocket.

"Blood?" He tenses, zeroing in the on the red drops feathered along the edge. He can't control his Protector instincts.

"Rough landing," I quickly say to calm him and hold up

my reddened palms as proof.

He faces me, takes each one of my hands, and kisses them gently at the wrist. "I despise that you've hurt yourself to visit me. I feel horrid."

"Don't. I'd do anything to see you."

"Yes, I recall you making a promise to stay home this summer. Why couldn't you have waited one more day?"

That's when the words to respond knot in my throat—the only words that will make breaking a promise worth it. *It's because I love you,* I want to say. But I can't. We haven't shared those feelings yet. I can't stand the thought of saying them out loud and not having him reciprocate. So those three weighted words stay in my heart—ones that I have never said to anyone. Not even to my own father.

"You know I can't follow rules." I make a joke instead.

"Oh yes, I'm quite aware."

He pulls me to stand, grabs my hand, and interlaces his fingers with mine. Electricity shoots through my arm, leaving a trail of prickly goose bumps. I lean into him, dropping my head on his arm, happy to be close after so long.

"What shall I do with you now?" he questions. "You've caught me off guard. Usually I have time to coordinate the perfect evening."

"I'm sure we can think of something. We're in London."

He's thoughtful, probably feeling the pressure to make everything as perfect as he always does. For some reason, I'm the one person he desperately feels the need to please.

"Just show me your favorite things to do," I suggest.

"Hmm, I think that might be terribly boring for you."

"Why?"

"I sit home, reading, most nights and pine over you."

I laugh. "Whatever." I nudge his body playfully. "I know you go out with your camera. Take me to your favorite places to photograph."

He leans down and whispers in my ear, "As you wish, my Seraphina."

His whispers of my name are the exact reason I'll never allow anyone else to call me by my full name—ever again. My entire body temperature warms, radiating from my ear. If I'm not careful, I'll melt like warm chocolate, right here in his arms.

After twenty minutes of strolling, we find ourselves inside the most exquisite restaurant. Spicy colors in saffron and deep, warm reds cover the walls. Hundreds of glass-patterned lanterns in rich turquoise and sapphire hang from wide wood beams. There are several archways of creamy marble, inlaid with intricate tile work. The aroma pulls me into the space even before the hostess greets us. I spin, inhaling the rich spices, only to open my eyes and see Bishop with his hand on his chin, smirking.

"What?"

"If I would have known I could have gotten this reaction out of you, we would have come here much sooner." He chuckles. "You're incredibly cute." He pulls me close and kisses my forehead, and then drops his hand to my lower back, guiding me forward.

The hostess seats us in a cozy, octagonal room on low chairs covered with feather-filled pillows. I reach out to stroke the silk curtains, billowing around. She rests menus on the table before bowing to leave.

"I've never eaten Moroccan before." I nervously glance over the menu.

"Don't worry, I'll order a little of everything. You'll love every bite."

Just then, a man in a white suit appears. He places two ceramic cups on the table and pours tea from a silverplated kettle with a long spout, curved like the neck of a swan. The kettle, reflecting the wall colors, hangs in his hand, high above the cups as he pours. He finishes without spilling a single drop. Then the attentive man tilts his body toward Bishop. "Would you like the usual, Mr. Bishop?"

"Yes, but surprise us with a few extra items, please."

"Yes, sir." The man ceremoniously bows, closes the surrounding curtains, and steps backward out of our private alcove.

"You *do* come here a lot." I smile and reach for the tea. I sip slowly, testing the temperature. Mint leaves swirl on the surface.

"I photograph food for their menus and website and then trade the photos for free dinners."

"Aren't you enterprising."

"It helps when you don't have money."

"Well, I guess that will change for us in a few weeks."

"Yes, the Oaths Ceremony will change everything," Bishop says thoughtfully. He plays with his napkin, eyes lowered.

The oaths are as ominous as they sound. It's the day that we dedicate our lives to the Society of Wanderers. It occurs in our junior year by no accident. They give you the first years to decide if this is the life for you—a trial period, of sorts. Since my goal is finding and saving my mom, I'm still in.

Some liken the ceremony to becoming a nun, but I think that's only half true. The part that's similar is that the Society hopes that you will feel a "calling" to serve. The part that's different is the lack of a vow of poverty and, thank goodness, chastity. Although, I haven't been lucky enough to worry about that last part yet. Bishop's a perfect gentleman in every unfortunate way.

The poverty part will be remedied by the large allowance that we'll receive weekly. This includes a new, loaded bank account, credit card, and unlimited access to whatever our hearts desire. In most students' eyes, the Academy just gets better and better. To me, their lavish gifts feel like a bribe.

"Are you nervous?" Bishop asks.

"A little." I squirm. "Most people don't have to decide their future when they're sixteen." I sigh. "What if I change my mind?" As soon as the words come out, I regret them. If I change my mind about being in the Society, that means I change my mind about being with Bishop, as his Wanderer, at least. And if I'm going to keep him, I need to be one hundred percent committed to our relationship and our Wandering team.

"I mean—" I stammer, looking for the right words, ones that won't hurt his feelings.

"It's okay, Sera. I understand. It's a lot of pressure to be someone you never knew existed until a year ago. It's a lot to absorb by anyone's standards." He smiles and reaches for my hand, comforting me. He turns my palm upward and traces the creases across the skin. His touch soothes, my shoulders drop, and I slouch into my feather seat.

"You're right." I smile.

Before long, plates piled with food in colors of gold, purple, green, and brown cover our table. Bishop explains each dish and watches me sample them. He laughs when I scrunch my nose with dislike for a few dishes.

When we finish dinner, Bishop wraps his arm around my waist and we step out from the sauna of rich perfumes and into the city streets. The air, cool and gentle, refreshes me.

We slowly make our way toward the embankment under a cloudy sky. A long string of light bulbs runs the length of the riverbank. Glowing hazes wrap like nests around each light.

Bishop tours me past his favorite photography spots. The Millennium Bridge, with its twisted steel, arches gracefully across the Thames River. We stroll past the Globe Theatre and Tate Modern Museum. He explains that he only visits to photograph people, tourists in particular. Farther away, he points out the National Theatre, set aglow with purple spotlights, and finally the Royal Festival Hall.

Our route winds inland for a short time and then through a tree-lined walkway toward the water. Shrouded in twinkling blue lights, a row of trees guides my eyes to the end of the park. Before us stands the very tall London Eye. The tallest Ferris wheel I have ever seen glows in beautiful ocean hues of aqua and cerulean. Enormous enclosed crystal capsules, instead of seats, rotate slowly around the outside of the wheel.

We reach the base and Bishop tugs me up the ramp.

"Uh, what are we doing?"

"I thought we'd take a ride."

"Bishop, I know you haven't seen me in a few months, but I doubt you've forgotten about my fear of heights." I giggle nervously.

He stops. "Sera, I'm your Protector. Trust me, please." His green eyes plead as he squeezes my hands.

Completely helpless against his will, I shrug, consenting, and halfway smile. He drapes his arm around my shoulders and drags me up the ramp. Bishop steps up to the ticket window and chats with the girl behind the glass. I mill around, farther away, holding my stomach in anticipation of the flips it will be taking.

Bishop's conversation ends with a chuckle. He turns. "Are you ready?"

"If this is really expensive, we should skip it," I suggest.

But really, it's my last-ditch effort to change his mind.

"Lucky for you, I know the girl behind the counter. We ride for free," he announces proudly. We step to the capsule entrance. The doors part to either side and he guides me in.

Anxious tingles spread from the heels of my feet, up my legs, and swirl around my stomach. I double over with a cramp and reach for his arm.

"Sera, we haven't even left the ground yet!" He pulls me to the center of the oval room toward a wood-slatted bench where we sit. "Just relax," he whispers and rubs my back.

I groan. "How do you know everyone in a city this large?" If he didn't know the girl, we wouldn't be riding for free. And just maybe, we wouldn't even be here.

"Old girlfriend." He smiles.

I stiffen. A hint of jealously flits around my brain. "Old girlfriend?" It's not like he isn't hunky enough to have those— probably *a lot* of those. Strangely, with our perfect relationship the notion never crept into my thoughts. But now, here it is, the aching sting of jealousy, ripe and ready for the picking.

"Don't worry, love. She dumped me," he consoles.

"What's her name?" I ask, attempting to hide the edge in my voice.

"Claire." He smirks. Clearly, he's enjoying my discomfort.

"How long ago?" I whisper, letting my gaze drift to the floor.

"About ten years."

I quickly calculate with confusion. "You would have been seven!"

"She was quite overwhelmed with choosing between Turner and me. He had a new red bicycle, and I just couldn't compete with my tattered roller skates."

We laugh together—I, for my stupidity, and he at me.

"I'm sorry," I say. "She just doesn't know what she's missed." Now I feel bad for Claire, who never knew the amazing person sitting next to me.

"Doesn't matter. I won the girl that matters." He leans in and traces his finger along my jaw, then nuzzles his nose at my ear. "My Seraphina," he whispers. His breath tickles my cheek. I squeeze my shoulders upward, pinching them to my ears, and giggle. I turn my back into his chest, and we meld into each other. When I look up, we're moving. I freeze.

"Here's the good thing about this ride." He snuggles closer around my now rigid body. "It takes thirty minutes to get all the way around—"

"That's not good!"

"I wasn't finished," he chides. "And we'll be completely *alone*." He wraps his arms around me. My stiffness diffuses. He pulls tighter. Playfully, his lips brush against my neck.

．

When we leave the London Eye, exhaustion consumes my body and my legs fail to function. I trip clumsily on my own feet. It's late, and I've been here for hours. And now, time-traveling jet lag—or *schlag*—is settling in quickly.

"I think it's time to go." I laugh and stumble, steadying myself on Bishop's arm.

"No, not yet. Come home with me, sleep a few hours, then you can leave."

A storm cloud opens and a flash of lightning cracks across the sky. Seconds later, we stand in a deluge of freezing rain. "I think I better go now."

We duck into a covered doorway.

"No way! You're staying. Besides, there's something I really need to talk to you about." Before I can respond, he tosses my arm over his shoulder and grabs my waist, propping me up.

"What?" I ask. A knot forms in my throat. A boy telling a girl that they "need to talk" is never, ever a good thing. My mind races; self-doubt edges in.

"Later, Sera. Just try to keep up."

Bishop and I step out into the open air, under the sweeping rain, and we run. With schlag taking over, I struggle to keep Bishop's pace. But what's worse is my mental hysteria over our relationship status. My internal hyper-anxiety battles with my need for sleep. One wins over and my eyelids droop closed.

Then, for no reason, the hair on the back of my neck stands on end. Something feels off. I lift my eyelids just enough to glance through the sheets of rain. Bishop's body tightens, rigid. We run to a nearby stone wall. He lays me down. Exhausted, I collapse on the pavement. He turns and crouches in a defense move we learned from class. *Something is wrong.*

Bishop's head twitches back and forth, peering out into the darkness. I attempt to stand, but the drops of rain transition into noisy sleet. Each pellet feels like a boulder, so very heavy, pushing me back to the ground. *Stupid schlag!*

"What's going on?" I holler.

"Quiet!" he hisses, holding up his palm.

Can he hear something I don't? I concentrate on the sounds: the pounding rain, beating like a drum over the pavement, cars hydroplaning on flooded streets, and the crackling lightning strikes. I advance beyond those noises, letting them float far away, and when I do, I actually hear a mass pushing through the rain.

By the time I look up it's too late. From behind the wall, a dark figure flies through the air above us. The person lands, crushing Bishop to the ground. Bishop flips the attacker off his body and the two launch into a full-force fight. They're equally matched, going back and forth between kicking at each other's heads and punching in dizzying repetition.

I've been practicing for months for this very moment, and now I'm utterly helpless because of the schlag. Hot fury rises through my bones. I attempt to stand again. Using all my strength, I inch my way up the wall.

I force my limbs to move and stumble forward, slamming into the attacker, hoping it will give Bishop the advantage. I must pass out momentarily because the next thing I register is my body being held by my feet as I'm dragged on my back across the sidewalk, arms flailing. My shirt and jacket lift, exposing my bare back. Rocks, dirt, and debris dig and slice into my flesh in the worst case of road rash I could ever imagine.

"Stop!" I scream over and over to my attacker.

My jacket slides over my face, blocking my sight and muffling my screams. I choke on the wet fabric. Now, no one can hear me cry. Finally, the jacket and shirt rip off, sliding over my arms, releasing me. My body halts.

Topless and in pain, I curl into a ball and cry as I'm pelted by the icy sleet.

"Sera!" Bishop rushes to my side. His fingers tremble over my bare skin. He tears off his jacket and gently rolls me into the fabric. He lifts my mangled body from the ground, and I float away, allowing the darkness to consume me.

№

8

SCHLAG

MUFFLED SHOUTS INTERRUPT MY SLEEP. WHEN I concentrate on the words, the person shouting says, "Bishop, breakfast!"

My eyes pop open even though I'm overwhelmed with exhaustion and pain. My gaze roams the unfamiliar room and then lands on an arm wrapped tightly around my stomach from behind. Bishop snuggles into my back, and I wince, feeling every scrape.

The nightmare from last night floods back: the rain, the fight, and oh man, *the talk*. I don't remember the last part taking place—yet.

Footsteps pound, ascending the stairs, and I jump out of bed, panicked. I've never met his mom before, and this definitely is not the way to do it. I lean over the bed and shake Bishop. "Wake up! Your mom's coming!"

He smiles with a lazy, unconcerned grin and rolls over. When his sleepy brain catches up, he jolts and reacts the way he should. "Right—that would be bad." He jumps up and scrambles for his shirt.

"Bishop. Are you awake?" she calls. Her steps and voice close in.

He runs to open the window, unlocks the bottom pane, and gives it a strong heave. Paint chips flutter to the sill, and he sticks his head out the window. He ducks in and turns to me as I finish shoving boots on my feet.

"This is going to be uncomfortable for you," he says apologetically. "There's a terrace and an iron fire escape ten feet away."

"Okay," I say, unsure. I quickly survey the room for other hiding options, but there are none.

"But you'll have to walk across the roof to get there." He winces.

I run to the window and look down. We're at least three stories up. *Ugg!* My stomach cramps, but I throw my leg over the sill, regardless. Leg dangling, a cool breeze blows past, sending chilly morning air beneath my skirt.

"She's almost here," he says. He wraps his arms around my body and helps me slide out the window and onto the slanted roof. My feet catch the brick rim, serving as a gutter at the edge of the shingles. I turn onto my side and securely clamp my fingers onto the window frame.

Bishop lets go when I'm stable, leans into his room, and quickly snaps the curtain sheers shut.

His bedroom door creaks open.

"Wonderful. You're awake," his mom says.

"Mum! You need to knock! I'm getting dressed." He positions his silhouette on the other side of the curtains, strategically blocking any view she might have of me.

"Of course. Sorry," she says.

The door shuts.

Curtains whip open and Bishop leans out to grab my arms. "Are you okay?"

"Umm," I reply with a shaky voice.

"Come back in. She's gone."

"No!" I yell a little too loudly. Not because I don't desperately want to get off this roof, but because I'm not ready to have *the talk*. "I'm already out here and—um—that's most of the battle." A bead of sweat rolls from my hairline and down my cheek. "Which way?"

His head tilts to my right, and I look over my shoulder. A rooftop veranda sits nearby. *I'm really going to do this. No sweat, just lean into the roof and step across the gutter. Easy—right?*

I inhale a long, shaky breath and unwrap my fingers, one at a time, from the window frame and reach to grab a nearby brick column with a decorative cement vase positioned on top. I gently roll to my hip, allowing one foot to rest in front of the other on the gutter. Slowly, carefully, I shuffle across the roofline.

Feeling unbalanced, I grab for a new shingle. At the touch of my hand, several pieces dislodge, sliding down the roof and tumbling over the edge. My entire body solidifies, except for my heart, which races, threatening to take off without me. The casualty of shingles crashes on the ground. I gasp, petrified.

"It's okay, Sera. You're almost there."

Taking several deep breaths, I reluctantly continue. Even in the chilly morning air, my entire body reeks of nervous sweat.

When I reach the end, I fall, relieved, into the veranda and rest on the patio, controlling my ragged breathing. Hoisting my body upright, I send Bishop a sad glance. My heart fills with dread, knowing that this may be one of the last moments we have as boyfriend and girlfriend. I'm certain "the talk" is the break-up talk. That thought makes this situation more upsetting. *How did we get here?* Our outing last night could not have been more perfect—until the end.

Bishop points to the back of the townhouse where two black metal bars attach to the roof and arc over the wall, disappearing over the edge.

I wave a feeble good-bye and traverse the patio. Grabbing the railing, I lean over the wall and look down. *Ugh!* I feel sick. A rickety metal ladder races down the side of the house. I don't dare jump over the edge to wander home; I can't gauge if there's enough room. I force another breath before a panic attack sets in and swing my legs over the edge for a second time this morning.

*

I don't leave London right away. Instead, I stalk around the city, working myself into a complete and utter frenzy by overanalyzing everything. I conclude that the "future me" I came across yesterday, the one crying, was the result of my impending breakup. I'm certain.

The person who attacked us last night, I'm not so certain about. If I hadn't been suffering from schlag, I may have had the energy to identify the person. I don't even know if Bishop knows who it was. I suspect not, since he didn't mention it. With his mom interrupting our peaceful slumber, we didn't talk about anything this morning.

The attacker stole my shirt and jacket. Ripped them right from my body with Bishop's letter in the pocket. *That beautiful, romantic letter—gone.* I'm thankful I committed the words to memory. When they race through my mind... *restless, waiting, dreaming,* the bridge of my nose burns. Tears begin again. I lift the oversized t-shirt, the one Bishop must have dressed me in last night while I was unconscious, and wipe my eyes and running nose. The skin on my face is raw and irritated, smeared with a tear-dried concoction of black mascara and face powder.

Ducking behind a row of tall, vibrant trees, I find a hidden stretch of green grass, a runway to return to the Academy. With one of my boots in hand as my relic and my ticket home, I run. The grass squishes mud between my bare toes as Battersea Park rolls up behind me into the sky. Right before the land crashes and bludgeons my body into oblivion, I catapult through a prismatic wormhole into time.

I land back in the attic of the Academy on my *true time*. A burst of light blinds me as I fly past the cast iron safe from yesterday. My arms and legs flail uncontrollably, and I smash into the person hindering my perfect landing.

As I'm laid out on the floor, a ring of sparkling dust withers in a mesmerizing haze above me. My wander dust, the residue of time travel, has turned a lovely iridescent shade of violet and brown. Gabe, the Academy's activities director, once explained that the colors are much like a mood ring. I wonder if violet and brown are the colors for sadness.

Exhausted with schlag and heartbreak, my body melts to the floor. The person whom I crashed into lugs himself from a jumbled pile of contrapulators. He stands over me with a scowl on his face.

Turner.

Figures.

"What the bloody hell are you doing, Sera? I nearly took your head off."

I groan, straining to lift myself to face him.

He reaches to help me from the floor, and I scream in pain.

"What have you done to your back? There's blood seeping through your shirt." He pauses and bends down to look me over. "I think I recognize this shirt," he huffs. "You've been with Bishop—haven't you?" He grimaces. "I swear he couldn't protect an armored truck!"

"Bishop," I whisper to myself. My eyes well up with tears. Turner lifts me from the floor with his strong arms and cradles me into his firm chest, somehow without touching my injuries.

"I need to take you to the nurse, so you better think of your alibi," he suggests and walks us out of the room to the emergency stairs.

"No," I plead through my pain. "My room. Please." I look up into his eyes, hoping he sees my suffering and understands that this misery extends beyond a mutilated patch of skin.

"Fine," he relents.

He carries me through the halls, looking down to inspect my face every so often. His features are similar to Bishop's but so different. Maybe it's his long dark hair or even his complexion that accentuates the deviation, or maybe it's his annoying attitude.

When he reaches my door, he nudges it with his knee and it flies open.

He carries me into my room and gently lays me on the bed. My butt touches the mattress first. Turner rolls me onto my side, careful not to touch the length of my back. My muscles relax into the mattress. He reaches and pulls off my remaining boot and tosses it on the floor.

"I need to look at your back."

"No!" I grunt.

"It's me or the nurse. You choose."

I roll my eyes. There's always an ultimatum with him. "Fine." I'm in no position to argue and too tired to care.

I roll onto my stomach. His shadow hovers. Carefully he rolls up my t-shirt. The fabric sticks to my back, ripping my skin as he pulls. I wince, and he stops.

"The blood's dried to the cotton in some areas. In others, it's still bleeding."

"Just leave it, please."

"Absolutely not. I'm beside myself that *he* didn't attend to this."

"Well, *he*—he was too busy thinking of a way to break up with me!" I bury my face into the pillow and cry uncontrollably. The schlag has made me irrational and hyperemotional. When the tears ease just slightly, Turner's laugh bellows through my bedroom. I glance at him in horror. *How is this funny to him?* "Stop it!" I yell; my feelings are hurt further by his rolling laughter.

"Sera, are you daft? My. God. Woman. He'll *never* break up with you!" He's laughing so hard now, tears stream down his face.

"He hasn't yet, but he will!"

"If that's why you are so sad, you shouldn't even waste your energy. You just don't get it, do you?"

"I guess not," I mumble to myself and pull my body into a sitting position.

Turner's raspy laughter recedes.

"You need to take a shower." He drags me to my feet.

"Not now, Turner. Really, I'm exhausted." My head falls to one side.

"Sera, you're a train wreck. You're bleeding, you're dirty, you're crusty, and you smell like an old sweaty rugby sock."

I narrow my eyes, and he smiles. Before I can decline again, he latches his hands on my shoulders and steers me to the bathroom.

"I'm not doing this with you here."

"Yes, you are."

He pushes away the shower curtain, lifts me into the tub, and leans me against the tiled wall. Then he adjusts the faucet and turns on the water. I jump in shock at the warmth. The deluge soaks my clothes. Water splatters my face.

"And I always pictured showering with you to be so much more fun." He laughs.

I find the energy to punch his arm.

"Ouch! Just kidding, love. I couldn't resist." He grins, happy with himself, and spins to leave, closing the door behind him. It creaks open again before I can move. "And I want to look at your back when you get out." He tosses a pair of pajamas inside. They land on the bathroom sink. "Someone's got to take care of you!" He slams the door, leaving for good this time.

No 9

UNEXPECTED RETURN

I'LL NEVER ADMIT IT, BUT FOR ONCE TURNER'S right. The shower makes me feel about twenty-five percent better. The other seventy-five percent is a lost cause. Only one person can rectify those losses.

I twist to look at my back in the mirror. My skin resembles ground hamburger meat. The elongated scrapes and gashes really do need medical attention.

I slip into my cotton shorts and slide on a button-down top, backward, leaving the back open like a hospital gown. It will be easier for Turner to look at my back and better if nothing touches it.

Turner relaxes on the couch with his feet up when I walk into the living room. Adjacent sits a tray of hot tea and a first aid kit.

"Feel better?"

I shrug, with no definitive answer, still traumatized by the thought of losing Bishop. One of Bishop's old letters sits on the coffee table, opened. Turner's been reading it. This annoys me to no end but, unlike other times, I don't have the urge to fight.

Turner hands me a cup of tea. "The caffeine will kill the schlag long enough for me to tape your back."

"Tape?"

"From what I saw, you would've been better off with a stitch or two in a few areas. But it's too late now. We'll have to use medical tape to pull the skin back together."

I finish my tea and sit next to him, facing away from his face. I pull my hair aside, letting it fall over one shoulder. His fingers lightly graze my skin as he folds each half of the shirt to the side to analyze the injury.

"How's it look?" I ask, already knowing the answer.

"Ghastly. What happened?" He picks up the bottle of antiseptic and cotton balls and continues working with a lithe touch. The liquid stings, but I try to be strong.

"We were in London, near Nine Elms, I think. It began to rain, and the schlag started getting to me. Bishop wanted to run to your house."

"Our house? Really?" He seems surprised.

"Yes, he wanted me to stay—*to talk.*" I tremble at the words but keep moving. "All of a sudden, he went all Protector-ish. He sat me on the ground and this person jumped him. They fought, and I tried to help."

"Of course you did." He rubs in more ointment.

"During the fight I must have passed out because the next thing I know, the attacker is dragging me across the pavement on my back." I cringe.

"Who was it?"

"Didn't see."

"What did they want?"

"I don't know. He—she—whoever took off with my jacket and shirt."

"Ah, I see. So someone attacked you and Bishop to render you topless. Pervert!" He chuckles.

I roll my eyes.

"What does Bishop think?"

"I have no clue. We haven't talked about it yet."

"Hmm." He doesn't elaborate on his thoughts, but I can hear the mental gears grinding.

His fingers stretch out several long strips of white tape. He bites each piece off with his teeth then places them firmly in selective spots on my skin.

"Done," he announces. He tosses the spool into the medical kit.

"Thanks." I turn to him.

Turner places his hand on my leg. His touch warms my

knee, causing tingles to radiate at the point of contact. Confused, I recoil. "Are you flirting with me? Bishop's gonna—"

"What? Now that he's breaking up with you he shouldn't care one bit if I make a play for his girl," he says seriously.

My lips turn down at the corners, and I look away, stifling a sob.

"Sorry. That was very insensitive." He turns my face to his and strokes a tear from my cheek with his thumb. "I promise, he will *never* break up with you."

"How do you know? You two don't talk—at all."

"I know because if you were mine, I'd never let you go." He looks at me with his intense gray eyes. They communicate silently, saying the words that can never be said out loud. Those implicit thoughts keep the air surrounding us thick with tension. Deep down, all along, I've known that Turner has feelings for me. His irritating ways are just his twisted attempts at flirting. I'm merely the schoolgirl with long pigtails, and he's the boy pulling them.

I look away. "Is that why you're being nice to me now?"

"I'm always nice to you."

"Really?" I pause and look at him. "Then give back my necklace."

"I will, when you explain what you're doing with it."

"I hope I'm not interrupting anything."

Startled, I look over my shoulder. Samantha James, my Seer, stands at the door in a blue suit that makes her look like a young Grace Kelly. She's grown half a foot taller over the summer, lengthening her already graceful posture.

"You're back early," I say, hoping she hasn't seen our silent exchange.

"Happy to see you, too, Sera." Sam glides forward. "This place looks like a disaster zone. I guess I can't expect anything more from you."

"Like I said, *you're early.*"

She leans onto the back of the couch, arms stretched wide to each side. Her eyes assess the lack of space between Turner and me. The two of them exchange a curt glance, and I quickly stand.

"What happened to you?" she says, now eyeing my back. "You two fighting again?" She smirks, knowing the typical turbulence between us.

"Really, I'm too tired to explain." I wrap my arms across the front of my body and walk to my room. I trip on a backpack sitting on the floor between the couch and the kitchen. The schlag's back. "Turner can fill you in." I yawn. "I'm going to bed."

*

When my eyes open, I know I've slept late into the next day. Dust flutters in the air near the window. Warmth of the afternoon sun beams into my room. A vacuum cleaner bangs against the wall in the living room, reminding me that Sam's home.

I'm happy for the schlag. Without it, I'm certain I would not have slept last night. My brain would have been too consumed with the uneasy events of the last twenty-four hours. On top of everything, Bishop's due back later today; this alone puts me on edge. I can't avoid him forever.

The vacuum turns off and a stereo flips on. Bach blasts through the apartment. "Air on the G String," Bishop's favorite. I'm sure Sam's irritating me on purpose—to wake me.

I drag myself off my stomach to a standing position then stumble for the door. I fling it open. "All right, I'm up! You can turn it down now!" I yell.

The music pops off. I look around for Sam, knowing she'll say something snarky. Instead, I see Bishop sitting on the floor with a screwdriver in his hand. He's fixing the doorknob.

"Sorry." He scurries to stand. "Sam told me you weren't here." He tosses the screwdriver in a toolbox.

How late is it? I glance at the clock in my room. Three thirty. I stand in shock as he crosses the room. He reaches out and rubs my shoulders with his hands and kisses my forehead. I can't decipher if the kiss is platonic, because my emotions have been rendered lifeless by my crying. If something has changed between us, I still don't understand why.

"What time did you get back?"

"About two hours ago."

"You came early." I avert my eyes.

"Yes, there's something we need to talk about, and it can't wait any longer."

My heart sinks. This cannot be it. I won't let it. "I—I—I—can't right now. I'm going to be late for an appointment with, um, Terease!" Yes, I'm supposed to be in her office by four.

"Okay." He pauses. "Are you feeling all right? Because you left in such a hurry the other morning, we really didn't get a chance to hash out what happened with the attacker. How's your back?"

"Great!" I gush. "But I really need to get a quick shower and get dressed. You know how Terease freaks if you're late."

"Okay, but promise me you will come straight back."

Nervously I shake my head. Having *the talk* is the last thing I want. I step backward into my room and shut the door in his concerned face.

Twenty minutes later, I run out the apartment, avoiding all eye contact with Bishop, then hurl myself down the hall.

The doors to the apartments are open, showing signs of life. Students roam about, congregating in familiar circles, recounting their summer activities.

When I reach the end of the hall and finally turn the corner into the main atrium, my body screeches to a halt. I stand, stupefied, looking at the person in front of me. Some-one I thought I'd never lay eyes on again.

№
10

AUNT MONA

Perpetua Gray leans against the wall
with her hand on her hip. Her steely eyes bore right
through me. Before I can react, she walks up and shoves me.
She grabs my shirt at the collar with tightened fists, muscling
me across the floor.

"Where's my crystal, witch?" she yells and forces me back
down the hall. She bashes me against the marble wall and I
cringe as my injuries scream at me. An eerie silence shoots
through the corridor. Every student turns to watch.

I glance down at her hands twisted into the shoulders of
my shirt. I look up at her and smile, taunting her, even though

I have absolutely no idea what crystal she's talking about. How does she even have the guts to show her snotty face here?

I know what I want to do, what I *can* do—destroy her. With my enhanced fighting abilities, I can trash her in a millisecond.

I whip my arm through the air, easily rotating her into a headlock. Perpetua screams, either from pain or from shock. I hope it's both. My foot swings, and I sweep her legs, dropping her body to the floor with a heavy thwack.

"Sera!" I instinctively look for the voice. Bishop races down the hall, moving at light speed. Immediately I let go of Perpetua, allowing her to regain the upper hand. Bishop can't see what I'm capable of—not yet.

She kicks the back of my knees, and I fall to the ground with the breath knocked out of me and I roll over. She pounds and beats at my chest, but Bishop tears her off before she can render too much damage. I scramble away, still huddled on the floor. He holds her, restraining her in a death grip. Students move closer to get a better view. Turner appears in the crowd, face flushed and clearly upset.

"Who let you back in?" I yell at her.

"Terease!" she spits. "I want my crystal back!" Bishop holds her elbows from behind. She pulls away from him, kicking ferociously in my direction.

Turner grabs my elbow, helping me up from the floor. At the small gesture, Bishop's eyes flicker a warning.

Bishop leans into Perpetua and whispers something. Whatever he says, it works, because she finally relents and stops fighting. Even still, her eyes say it all. Wherever this crystal is, the one she thinks I have, it's important.

"Let me go." Perpetua jerks away from Bishop. Now free, she shoots me a murderous look. Without another word, she twirls and stomps away, marching down the hall, and enters her old apartment. Her team—Stu, her Wanderer, and Jessica, her Seer, follow her. The door slams shut behind them.

My mouth hangs open at the realization that she's back. Her entire team is back! The Academy has readmitted them. Terease readmitted them! Even after they tricked Bishop and me into a meeting with the Underground, where we almost died last semester.

"What did you say to her?" I look at Bishop in confusion.

"I simply told her you don't have her crystal." His gaze swings from me to Turner and hardens. "Don't you have a meeting with Terease?" he snaps.

"Yes." I nod and hurry away.

I charge down the sweeping stairs, through the grand atrium, past the indoor pool, and into the maze of teachers' offices. Terease's office sits behind a glass-plated wall. Unable to control my temper, I bang on the glass before I stalk in. She's in a meeting with two men dressed in black suits.

"You let Perpetua, Stu, and Jessica back into school? Are you out of your flippin' mind?" I point at her, my lower lip trembles with hatred. Crossing Terease in this manner means you have a death wish.

She rises from her desk, nostrils flaring. "Leave us!" she yells to the men. They jump from their seats, examining me with curious expressions as they go.

"Sit!"

I pace for a second, burning off more fury. Finally, when I think a chair can contain my anger, I sit.

"I know you will find this hard to believe, but I wanted to tell you she was returning before she got here. That's why I asked you to my office today."

"How can you even think it's a good idea to let her back in? Any of them?" My blood rushes toward my hands, where I'm clenching the desk's edge.

Terease sits down, taking her time to answer. She swivels to face the wall, glancing at TV monitors. They feed video from the security cameras, the E.Y.E.S. She spins again, her silky cropped hair flinging around with her as she does.

"The Academy was able to, shall we say, secure certain information that will lead us to Cece and the Underground. And that information is worth quite a lot." Her red lips turn up at one corner.

"And what does that have to do with Perpetua?" I cross my arms and stare.

"Perpetua exchanged information on Cece's whereabouts for her and her team's return to the Academy."

"You let her bribe her way back into school?"

"Call it what you want." Her lips purse.

I stop to consider the information. If Terease knows Cece's location, then she knows my mom's. Maybe I won't need the rosary necklace after all.

"I want in," I blurt.

"What?"

"When you go to find her. I want to be there," I say plainly. I know Terease will want to be the one to drag the redheaded, blood-loving freak in, and I want to be there too.

Terease bites her long black fingernail and rotates to the TVs as though she's considering my offer. After several moments she simply says, "No."

"What!" I jump to my feet.

"I said, no!" she repeats. "Now, leave." She waves her hand but never turns to face me. She only leans into one of the pictures dancing across a monitor, hoping to catch someone doing something they shouldn't.

I consider telling her that Perpetua just beat me up, but I know it won't do any good. Angry, I bolt through the hall, and march right out the front doors of the Academy. If Terease can admit Perpetua back into school, she can admit me a free pass out of this place—alone.

As I leave, racing down the front stairs, I glance over to the mirror school. The west Washington Square Academy, the one for the *Normals*. They have absolutely no clue how lucky they are to be just that—normal. And for the first time since I learned that I'm a Wanderer, I wish I were normal too.

I run out of the courtyard, past the obelisk, with no particular destination in mind. Physical activity helps release my anxieties. Thankful that I put on tennis shoes, I open my stride, running and pushing my muscles. I inhale the September Chicago breeze and decide not to look back, at least for a few hours.

Running around the city allows me to feel ordinary. I think about things that I generally don't when I'm locked away in the inner sanctum of the school: the smell of pizza, parents playing with their children in the park, cars sitting in traffic, a shopkeeper sweeping his front walk, and music.

Even music, the thing that I loved most in my "Normal" life has taken a backseat to my Wandering life. The urge to write, to sing, to create a melody are gone. Finding my mom, being a Wanderer, becoming a better fighter, Bishop, and every other high school drama consumes my mind. There's no place for music now. The speed at which my priorities in life have changed scares me. What will I be a year from now? Ten years? Will I even recognize myself?

When I return to school, it's three hours later. I calculate that I've run at least the length of a marathon, maybe more. Somehow, in the last several months, my physical prowess has changed, along with my heightened emotional volatility.

I walk around the golden obelisk in the school's courtyard. I reach my arms high above my head and shake out my legs. Unfortunately, no amount of stretching will save me from the world of ache I'll feel tomorrow. I bend over and touch my toes, feeling the scabs on my back pull and crack.

Sensing someone staring, I glance at the East Academy. Bishop stands at his bedroom window, looking out, his face expressionless. One hand rests on the window frame. He doesn't wave or acknowledge that our eyes have met. He only turns and disappears from view, letting the curtains drape closed.

I can't run away from him forever. And if he's bent on breaking up, I'll have to accept it. The run has given me some clarity, allowing a peaceful place for my emotions to be dealt with in a logical way. If he doesn't want to be with me, it's not healthy for me to want to be with him. It's that simple. I'm only sixteen, with my whole life ahead of me. Will I really die if a stupid boy breaks up with me?

I consider this and look at Bishop's window. My nose burns again, but I push away the waterworks. Yes, yes, it might kill me, and I'm certain I can't handle it, at least not at this very moment. So I keep moving, walking to a place I know I can find sanctuary—Aunt Mona's house.

A few blocks away, I stroll past the front hedges and into the miniature yard of the Victorian townhouse. I squat, feeling under Mona's mosaic-covered garden sculpture. A silver key lays among the earthworms and beetles, resting in the damp earth. I scoop it up and head for the front door.

After I enter, I kick off my sneakers in the vestibule and step into the main living area. A pile of mismatched tapestry suitcases lay on the floor. Aunt Mona's back from her painting trip in Europe.

"Mona!" I yell, my voice echoing through the lofty living space.

"Oh, darling!" Mona rushes in from the kitchen with a smile

across her face. She tucks a strawberry-blonde lock behind her ear, right before she throws her bony arms around my back. She offers me a kiss on each cheek then holds me away from her body.

"Your face is flushed red!"

"I just went for the longest run of my life."

"Funny, I don't remember you being a runner when I left." Her brow furrows in confusion.

"Helps to relieve stress. I've got lots these days." I try to smile. I forgot how easy it is to open up to her. In my mind, I'd always hoped that she and my mom were very similar in this way. They had to be, being sisters and all.

"Come in, I'm making dinner," Mona says. I follow her to the kitchen.

"*You*—making dinner—the real kind?" I balk.

"Well, I decided to expand my horizons this year. Not only did I paint in Italy, I took an exquisite cooking class!"

"Sweet! So what's on the menu?"

"Pasta alla Norma." She drops an apron over her head, securing the ties behind her neck and her waist.

Mona pours herself a large glass of red wine and a soda for me. I sit on a stool at the island across from her. I grab the butcher block, knife, and vegetables. Taking an eggplant, I slice off the ends and then cut it longways into thin slices.

"So what's the drama?" Mona asks, then swirls her wine in its glass. She holds the rim to her nose, inhaling the aromas before taking a small sip.

"You wouldn't be interested." I shrug, looking at my eggplant.

"Try me." She expertly rips basil leaves from their stems.

"Well, for one, Terease readmitted Perpetua and her team."

"Really? What would compel her to do such a horrid thing?"

"Perpetua seems to have some information on Cece's whereabouts." I peek up to gauge her reaction.

"Really? Well, that would be wonderful if the Society could finally do away with her." She throws some fresh pasta into the boiling water on the stove. "How do you feel about it?" A typical Mona question, always pushing to explore my feelings.

"I can't say that it thrills me." But if there's a possibility it will help find my mom, I think I can live with it.

"And what else is going on?" she asks, and reaches for a clove of garlic. She pounds it with the flat side of a large knife. The skin cracks open, and she peels the outer layer.

I fail to find the correct words to explain why I believe Bishop's going to break up with me without sounding like a pathetic, angst-ridden teenager. So I just blurt it out. "Bishop's breaking up with me!" I drop my head into my hands, but I don't cry. I'm too dry to make anything else come out.

"What? That's absurd."

"It's true. He said that we 'needed to talk.' And everyone knows what that's code for."

"Yes, I believe I do. It's code for we need to talk about the weather, about how glorious I think you are, about how I need help with this new fabulous Protector defense move. Sera, there's just no way for you to know what he wants until you actually have *the talk*." Her voice drops, low and dramatic.

She makes everything sounds so simple. But I'm not buying it. Bishop and I spent an entire evening together. No topic would have been off limits—except a break-up talk.

Mona might deny the truth behind the words, regardless. She loves Bishop, I think even more than she loves me. It's okay because having her approve of my boyfriend makes my life easier. She's a valuable ally, if and when Ray ever finds out about him. Because when he does, it won't be a pretty day. When Ray finds out Bishop and I are dating *and* living in the same apartment—well, he'll explode. We can't easily explain our special scenario to Ray, a mere *Normal*.

Mona walks around the counter and delivers a reassuring hug. "You are a beautiful, intelligent young lady. Bishop would be insanely stupid to break things off with you. I truly believe that you're jumping to conclusions. And you know there's only one way to find out."

"Yes, I know. Just face him." The looming fear of it is driving me crazy. I think I'm ready to just deal with the consequences, whatever they may be.

Time with Mona is exactly the sanctuary of normalcy I need. She fills me in on her travels over the best Pasta alla

Norma I have ever shoveled into my mouth. She, it seems, is a natural cook. Then she shows me her photos over dessert—a chocolate cannoli.

When I return to the Academy, most of the dorm doors in the hall are shut, signaling their occupants have turned in for the evening.

Even though I tell myself I'm ready to do this, I half hope that Bishop will be asleep. Our apartment door sits slightly ajar, and I walk in. A dimmed gas lantern flickers light over the kitchen counter. Both Bishop's and Sam's doors are closed.

Now I just need to walk across the floor without making it creak. I step slowly, seeking out steps on the area rug where available. It helps to muffle the sound. Then I step from the rug to the kitchen floor.

When I'm standing in front of my bedroom door, I finally breathe a sigh of relief, feeling happy that I have one more night. I'm such a coward. After this mess, I promise myself to be stronger.

I push through my door, kick off my shoes, and switch on the light next to the bed. And that's when I scream.

No 11

THE TALK

BISHOP JUMPS, AWAKENED OUT OF A SLUMBER. His body tenses but relaxes when he sees it's me. He throws his hand across his forehead, blocking the light and rubs his sleepy eyes.

"You ruddy well scared the hell out of me."

"Sorry, I wasn't expecting you to be here," I say, my heart racing.

He sits up, still half asleep, and pushes himself farther back on the bed to make room for me. He pats the sheets with his palm. I sigh. *This is it. I can't run any longer.*

"Where have you been? I thought you were coming back

to the apartment after your meeting?" He yawns.

"I was, but then I decided to go for a run."

"Is that why you stink so badly? You've been running for——" he squints at the clock, "for eight hours."

"I went to Mona's too."

"I see." He's quiet for a moment. "Why don't you take a shower? I'll wait for you."

"Okay," I mumble. I push off the bed and disappear into the bathroom. When I'm done, feeling refreshed but solemn for what's about to happen, I walk across the room and crawl into bed. With Bishop behind me, he wraps his arm around my waist, and then he tucks his chin into the curve of my neck.

"Why do I feel like you've been avoiding me since I returned?" he asks quietly. "Is everything okay?"

"I don't know, you tell me," I say with a clip. He doesn't respond. "I mean, I guess I've been avoiding you because I wasn't ready for *the talk*." My voice shakes, instantly activating the tears. I wipe my nose with the sleeve of my robe.

"The *talk*?"

"You know, the talk where you break up with me." I frown and look at his arms wrapped around me, strong and perfect.

"Break up with you?" He snorts. "Why on earth would you think that?"

I inhale and turn to face him in the same motion. "If you aren't, then why did you say we needed to talk?"

"Wait, back up a second. How can you even think that's a

possibility? Has something happened between us that I don't know about?" His brows pull together.

"No, but—I—" I can't think of what to say because my brain, my heart, my lungs, every part of my body feels a surge of relief—a new sense of elevated hope.

"Seraphina Parrish, you are utterly and ridiculously cute. I promise that I'll never, ever tell you that we need *to talk* again."

"Please don't!" We laugh together. Even still, a few more tears escape in a rush of happiness.

He kisses my nose and then stretches his arms tightly around me. I grimace. "Sorry, my back's still a little tender."

"I wanted to talk to you about that, too."

"Who was it?" I ask.

"I've been thinking about it, and I have no idea. It's not like they robbed us of money. And I'm quite certain it was another Wanderer. I tried to bandage you up that night, but you wouldn't allow me near you."

"I don't remember that." I attempt to retrieve the memory but come up blank.

"You were quite agitated. I could only talk you into putting on a shirt and sleeping. It must be a side effect of the schlag," he considers.

"Don't worry, Turner fixed me up when I got home."

Bishop tenses. "How did *Turner* happen to be your savior?"

I cringe, wishing I hadn't said that. "It's a long story," I brush it off.

"I'm listening," he says, propping himself up on his elbow.

I explain how I wandered home into the attic, crashing into Turner, and how he brought me to the apartment, cleaned my back, and added bandages. Bishop flinches every time there's a possible situation in which Turner touches me. I leave out the part where he grabs my leg. No sense in upsetting him further.

"You two have been spending some time together, then?" His brows wrinkle.

"No—I mean—not really—a little," I confess. "But seriously, he's pretty annoying. I'm not sure how you stand him sometimes," I add to make him feel better, and also because it's true. "I know you don't like each other, but he *did* help me."

"Yes, and I will have to pop over to thank him for that." He seems to relax, so I snuggle into his chest. He rubs his fingertips the length of my bare leg, leaving a trail of tingles in their wake.

"So what is it you wanted talk about?" I test the waters, feeling the topic's safe now.

Instead of responding, he leans close and gently kisses my neck. His mouth traces the length of my jaw until his warm lips find mine. Together, they glide softly back and forth. The kiss sends a firestorm of desire racing through my body. Pulsating heat begins at my mouth, pools in my stomach, and shoots out through my curling toes.

His warm breath penetrates my skin, swirling and surging into my heart, which beats wildly out of control. His lips urgently move around my neck and retrace my shoulder. His hand slips under the hem of my shirt. His other quickly follows, and together, both hands slide down my waist and latch on to my hips, then he tugs me forward, locking my body against the curve of his.

For the first time ever, Bishop's losing control. Up until this point, he's treated me with the same care one takes with a porcelain doll—one that will break if hugged too tightly. Shocked by his new aggressiveness, I nudge him away.

"This isn't talking, you know?" I whisper.

"Believe it or not, it has to do with what I want to talk to you about," he says, breathless.

"Tell me." I seductively trace the outline of his collarbone with my fingertip.

"That whole night in London, Seraphina, I wanted to tell you. I wanted to find the perfect moment. I tried, but I couldn't make the words come out." He speaks slowly, as though unsure of himself.

He grabs my hand and kisses the palm before placing it cupped over his stubble-covered cheek. "But now I just can't wait any longer." His gaze falls on mine, and even in the moonlit room, I can see the sparkling ocean of green in his eyes. "I love you." He breathes in relief.

"And I love *you*," I respond quietly. My lips broaden into a smile. I've wanted to tell him the same thing for months. All this time, we felt the same way, having the same apprehension. The whole "talk" thing seems so stupid and childish now and so very far away in my mind.

Bishop kisses me again. I drop my arms over his shoulders and wind my fingers into his shirt. All my emotions take over, solidifying every piece of my heart that I thought would surely be broken tonight. Instead, it pounds stronger, and more in tune with his. It begs me to melt and disappear into his body, breathe him in, and clutch him closer. I drop my hand to his chest, where his heart pounds chaotically beneath my fingertips.

We're feverishly kissing, tangled, wrapped, rolling, and squeezing against each other. My entire body rushes with a torrent of wild energy, overwhelmed by this new surge of eagerness on his part. There's a frenzy of ecstasy in every thoughtful touch and every insignificant brush of his trembling hand on my skin.

Bang, bang, bang. The wall shakes.

We quickly unhinge ourselves from each other, falling away, breathless. Sam isn't asleep. And unfortunately for us, she can see what Bishop sees, an uncomfortable side effect of being a team. Protectors and Seers can tap into the other's minds and eyes without notice, whenever they want. I believe that's why Bishop stays on his best behavior, because he never knows when Sam will stop by mentally to say "hi." He won't allow someone he regards as a little sister to see more than hand-holding.

"Did you know she was awake?" I ask, embarrassed.

"She wasn't a few moments ago, I checked. In fact, she was happily dreaming of winning a spot in the Joffrey Ballet," he says, sliding a finger beneath the edge of my robe, teasing my skin.

I giggle. "But all this time, I didn't know you could see each other's dreams, too."

"We try not to. In fact, we try to block each other out as much as possible. It's harder in the beginning. It's sporadic and, at times, uncontrollable. But hopefully we'll have a handle on it before too long." He smirks suggestively and steals a lingering kiss before we receive another bang on the wall.

Bishop snores lightly next to me, a delightful purr. I nuzzle into his chest and breathe deeply. I'm amazed that he smells this wonderful all the time.

Someone quietly knocks on my bedroom door. "Sera," an annoyed voice says from the other side.

I roll out of bed and slide into my silk robe while walking across the room. I crack open the door, just enough to peek my nose through.

Sam stands on the other side, her arms folded across her chest. With a disapproving look, her eyes appraise my bed head and attire.

"You have a visitor." Her head jerks to one side.

Turner stands in the open doorway, arms stretched high above his head, leaning into the doorframe. His arms look even more muscular that way. The nerves in my stomach swirl in a wild swarm of butterflies. I step out and shut the door tightly. Bishop will die if he finds out that Turner's paying me visits. Sam moves aside, watching me shuffle across the room, gathering my messy hair into a low bun.

"That's not going to help," she snaps. I turn to give her a nasty look.

"What's up?" I ask him.

"I just wanted to stop by and tell you those new *things* you requested are ready." His flirtatious eyes gaze from under his lashes.

He's talking about my new defense holograms.

"I thought you weren't going to do them?" I cross my arms.

"Well, I've reconsidered." He smirks.

I lean into him and whisper, "Well, in that case, are you going to give my other *thing* back?"

He shakes his head, giving me a cynical look.

A door creaks open behind me.

"What are you doing here?" I turn. Bishop stands at my bedroom door, half-asleep but still managing to look furious. Turner shifts uneasily, assessing the situation. He scrutinizes Bishop, standing outside my bedroom door, and then his troubled eyes fall on me, surveying and deciphering my face. I've quickly read his mind. It's easy to see where his over-sexed thoughts have led him. Immediately uncomfortable, I wrap my robe tighter around my body, fists gripping the fabric closed. Blood rushes to my cheeks, and my gaze drops to the floor.

"Hello, my good brother. It's nice to see you, too." Turner feigns a smile. The two lock gazes; a storming hatred of tension courses between them.

Turner releases the confrontation first and then holds up something. "Actually, I came by to give you back your boot. You must have dropped it the other day when you returned from...London, was it?" He shoots Bishop a peevish look.

"Yes, thanks," I say, grabbing it quickly, giving him a pleading look, one asking him to leave before things get ugly. Turner maintains his macho demeanor, but I know he's hurt. Ignoring Bishop, he sharply nods to Sam and me and then turns to stalk away. He tips his head to my best friend Macey as she rushes past him in the hallway.

Macey's wide, bouncing curls rain over my face as she grabs and pulls me in for a hug. I haven't seen her since last semester. She skips the hellos, processes our apartment, and delves right into the gossip. "Why is Bishop standing in your bedroom door, looking like he just rolled out of bed? *Your* bed?"

"That's for me to know," I whisper, knowing it will set her off.

"Bull crap!" She captures my hand, yanks me down the hall, dragging me through her apartment, past her team hanging out, playing video games on the sofa, and into her bedroom. She slams the door and runs to jump onto her bed, bouncing like a child.

"You little vixen. Tell me everything," she explodes, clasping her hands in front of her chest.

"There's nothing to tell." I feel a blush stealing over my cheeks, belying my words.

"There's something. I can see your new womanly glow. Now get over here and spill!"

I jump onto the bed, a little excited with my news. "What you're thinking, it didn't happen. But—"

"But what?" Macey's eyes are so large and round, they may bug out of her head.

"Last night, he said he loves me!"

"Aww." Macey grabs a pillow and hugs it to her chest. "Nothing else?" Her eyes narrow.

"Nope, I promise."

"What about *that* Turner? He's a hottie!"

I shrug slightly, saying neither yes nor no to the observation. But how can Bishop's own brother not be beautiful. It's impossible.

"He's a pain," I say, trying to dispel her awe.

"Who's he dating?"

"Why, Miss Du Bois, are you saying you've got the hots for Mr. Turner Bishop?"

"With all that thick hair and those muscles?" She sighs dramatically and flops backward onto the bed. Reclining, she props herself on her elbows. "He's definitely easy on the eyes, but no. Unfortunately, I'm still navigating my own relationship time bomb."

Macey has two suitors, Xavier Blackburn and Quinn

Hayes, both of whom are her team members. It's an uncomfortable situation.

"In my mind, I'm crazy about them both, but I just can't commit to either." She huffs.

"Do you mean you can't, because you can't decide, or you don't want to hurt someone's feelings?"

"Both. I think." Her face scrunches in contemplation.

"They're both madly in love with you, ya know?"

"I know, I know. They drive me crazy. A good crazy, I think. Boys are so confusing. I don't know what to do. Let's talk about something else," she reels off quickly.

"I heard about that Perpetua giving you crap yesterday. If I were here, I would have kicked the pretty off her face for you," she says.

"Thanks." I smile. It's nice to have Macey back. I too wish Bishop wasn't around yesterday, so I could have just kicked Perpetua's pretty face myself.

At the thought, I remember that there are new holograms to practice with. Even with all this teen drama, I need to practice if I'm ever going to take care of my real problem—hunting down Cece and the Underground and saving my mom.

№ 12

HOLOGRAMS

A FTER DISCUSSING THE NUANCES OF CHOOS-
ing the perfect boyfriend with Macey for two hours, I
finally head back to my room. A train of garment racks rolls
down the hall and stops at the end of the corridor.

I squeeze past them and into my apartment. Gabe Garcia,
the activities director, stands in the middle of our living room.
He chats with Sam and Bishop, arms flailing with animated
gestures. I catch the tail end of his elaborate story, something
about his buying exploits in London, New York, and Paris over
the summer vacation. Every year he buys each student a completely new wardrobe, compliments of the Academy.

"Sera!" Gabe screeches with excitement. "Love it, love it, love it!" he says as he touches my hair, my chin, and gestures at my robe. "It's so bed-head chic." He waves his hands through the air.

"Now, I was just telling Bishop and Samantha that I'll be changing out your wardrobes this afternoon for the new year. So I want you all to make yourselves scarce for a few hours."

"You really don't need to do this," I say. As much as I adore fashion, it seems a horrible waste.

"Don't worry, my little poppy seed. We'll be donating all the old clothes to charity. Every shirt, every ruffle, every everything! The needy will just be bursting with glorious chiffon, velvet, leather, and sequins, but hopefully not in that combination!" He sniggers. Gabe pinches my cheek, then turns and goes to work.

Bishop leaves the Academy to run errands. Samantha spends the afternoon in Olde Town with her ballet instructor and then her cello teacher. I change into workout gear and head to one of the personal training rooms, where no one will bother me and I can kick the crap out of one of my new defense holograms.

I jump on the nearby elevator. The ancient cage closes, and I rotate the rusty lever. The box glides down the elevator shaft into Olde Town. When it slams to the ground, I return the lever to its original position, retract the cage door, and step out.

The Animates here, metal raptors, occupy high pedestals on either side of the entrance bridge. With aviary precision, they twitch their heads, cocking them sideways, studying my approach with their bulbous yellow eyes. Internal cranks screech and grind as they move. One raptor stretches its long neck into the water rushing below the bridge and pulls out a flopping fish. The bird's beak tilts upward and the fish drops into its throat. *Strange. Wouldn't their diet consist of oil or something?*

When I cross the drawbridge into the city, the temperature is neither hot nor cold. The courtyard, vibrant with life again, smells of smoldering wood. Students mill about, making me realize how lonely I was all summer.

I stroll past the Tower Building with the clock on its facade and into a dark archway that winds away beneath it. After several hundred paces, the vintage lantern at the entrance of the Defense Arts training rooms sputters to life.

The wooden door with iron findings slides open to a room as big as a gymnasium. Wood pillar posts support the high-reaching ceiling. Rusted chandeliers hang from long chains in three spots above, casting reflections onto the glossy wood floor. The decor style resembles a mix of old castle and high school basketball court. When school starts again on Monday, students will train here in the art of fighting.

The rooms I prefer to use flank both sides of the gym. They're smaller, with foam-padded floors and mirrored walls. But most importantly, they're private. I use the room farthest away. Turner has equipped that one with the defense hologram machines. It's also the room students use the least, where I'm less likely to be found.

My sneakers squeak as I walk across the waxed floor. The door to my private room detects a presence as I near and slides open. I walk through and it glides shut. The industrial lights buzz and flicker to life.

I step into the middle of the room to stretch. After a few lunges and toe touches, my gaze locks onto the mirror. I practice intimidating expressions that I might give an attacker. When I've sufficiently riled myself up, like some kind of football player before a big game, my excitement surges at the thought of fighting a new hologram. I'll have to thank Turner later, secretly.

"Seraphina Parrish. Hologram on," I say to activate the four machines mounted around the room. Their green lights blink, ready for the next command.

"Defense hologram number thirty-seven," I say the words slowly and clearly. Thirty-seven will be the newest routine. I hope Turner programmed something monstrous.

The machine speaks back, confirming the routine. "Hologram number—thirty-seven. This routine requires—no weapons. Safe words are—'you win,'" the machine intones in a robotic voice. The safe words will end the routine, turning the machine off.

One minute later, a countdown begins. At the end, a hologram appears out of a vibrating haze of electrified dust. The vision, facing away, solidifies into a humanlike mass, then turns.

The boy stands six feet tall, a foot taller than myself. This in itself isn't a big deal; I've fought taller. When he looks at me with eyes that look almost blue today, I don't know if I can truly fight him, because the hologram looks exactly like Turner.

I evaluate him. My face flushes with embarrassment at his shirtless physique. His workout pants hang low, barely grazing his hipbones. My gaze wanders up his chiseled torso as he confidently strolls forward. That's when I see something that makes me want to scream. My black rosary swings from his neck, brushing his sculpted pecs.

Hologram Turner stops. "See anything you like?" he asks amusingly and looks down at himself. I roll my eyes at his pathetic cockiness. He reaches for the rosary, holds it up, examining it.

"I'll make you a deal." The hologram paces, sputtering electricity. "If you can beat me in a match, I'll give you your necklace back. But not until then." He grins. "Until then, it'll stay right here." He pats his chest. "Right next to my heart."

A rage builds inside. At the chance of winning the necklace, I don't even give him an opportunity to finish his thoughts. I charge clear across the room, blazing with fury.

Turner doesn't expect me to fight him. I know because there's a flash of surprise behind his eyes when I collide with his body, knocking him to the floor. I reach to rip the rosary off his neck, but he grabs my wrist first, halting it in midair. He's stronger for sure, so it won't be easy to win.

He uses the momentum of the struggle to roll me over

until we've switched positions. He straddles my waist, my hips locked between his thighs. Both my wrists are above my head, secured against the floor. My struggling only makes him smile.

He leans in close to my face so that we're sharing the same air. I want to turn my face to the side to avoid eye contact, but it would only be a sign of weakness, and I have to at least appear stronger than him.

"Not going to be as easy as you thought, is it?" he says with a crooked smirk.

"Sure it is." I smile, and then head butt him.

Hologram Turner falls away, instantly releasing me to grab his forehead. I scramble to my feet, and he quickly recovers and does the same.

"That was a cheap shot!" he shouts.

"It's not going to be as easy as you thought, is it?" I jab playfully.

This time he doesn't respond, but I can see he enjoys the banter as much as I do. He crouches defensively, but after we circle each other a few times, I can see that he won't attack first. That would not be the gentlemanly thing to do.

I twist sideways with my weight on one leg, then lash out to kick his stomach. He grabs my foot before it makes contact and throws it aside. Without missing a beat, I kick him again. Punch. Punch. Jab. Push. Kick. He only responds to block me, like some kind of lame punching bag.

I bounce away from him, out of striking range. "Well, you're not being any fun! Fight back!"

He crosses his arms.

"I knew it, you're scared! Ha!" I tease.

"Hardly!" He laughs. "You're five feet tall and eighty pounds."

"One hundred and seven and all muscle," I correct and throw a few punches in the air.

He waves me forward with his fingertips.

I smile, strangely excited, and advance with another blow. This time he responds, taking a swipe. I duck and punch him back.

Our hand-to-hand fight is fierce, slightly hot, and completely unrelenting. An hour passes and I've finally, which much difficulty, coerced him into a submissive headlock. I'm about to finish the fight, to win the necklace, when the room's door suddenly slides open.

"You win!" I scream and release him to quickly turn off the hologram machine.

Hologram Turner turns and whips my body to the floor and stands above me. His smile gleams with triumph, right before his body dissipates, rolling away into the air in blue electrical flakes.

Completely annoyed, I roll over to see who has entered. If they hadn't, I'd have won the necklace by now.

Volta Swift, my Defense Arts instructor, stands at the door. Everything about the woman is striking, from her dark skin that contrasts sharply with her short and spiky white hair, to her muscular body, and her eyes…especially her eyes. She's the only person I've ever met whose blue eyes edge into the realm of violet, like mine.

"The professor said you might be here." She walks across the floor and helps me up. "Did you win?"

"No, unfortunately."

"That's too bad. The professor mentioned that you've been working very diligently this summer with his new invention."

I hope he hasn't mentioned it to anyone else. Although I know that the teachers don't consort with students, so the ones who are privy to my intensified defense lessons—like Terease, the professor, and Ms. Swift—wouldn't say anything to Bishop. They'd have to go out of their way to do so. The real problem is Turner.

"I came to see one of the machines in action for myself. Do you mind if I have a go at it?"

"Go ahead." I gesture to the floor.

I stand against the wall as she walks into the middle of the room. She activates the machines by her name.

"Volta Swift," she says clearly. The machine scrolls noisily, looking for advanced holograms that have been programmed especially for her. "I'd like to use the holograms for training this year," she speaks over her shoulder.

"Holograms found," the robotic voice announces. "Hologram number—one— requires—a sword. Safe words are—'you win.' You have—one minute to retrieve your weapon. Countdown starts in—one minute."

Ms. Swift walks calmly across the room and chooses a

sword from the overflowing weapons rack. She inspects the blade, flipping it from one side to the other.

"Starting in—thirty seconds," the machine intones.

Ms. Swift walks to the center of the room, swiping the sword through the air several times.

"Starting in—ten seconds."

I slide my back down the wall and stretch my legs out before me, anxious to see her in action. Until now, the professor, Turner, and I have been the only ones to use the holograms.

"Hologram number—one—starting now." The machine beeps five times. Through a cloud of haziness, a ten-foot-tall, two-headed, dragon beast-man appears in front of her. I jolt slightly. The beast is more hideous than anything I've ever fought. Ms. Swift crouches. The smile on her face reflects in the surrounding mirrors. In some sick way, she probably finds this fun, much like I do.

The beast man whips its long necks around the ceiling. Clutching his sword with his puke-colored scaly claw, his lizard eyes zero in on Ms. Swift, and he squares his body. Hulking forward, his sword swipes at the air in unison with his two bobbing heads. The beast spits a raging fire across the room and Ms. Swift stops and expertly dives out of its searing path.

The fight is a dance. Ms. Swift's athletic grace carries her as she methodically carves chunks of scaly flesh from the beast's body. With each slice, yellow blood the consistency of mustard spews from its wounds, eventually covering the entire floor. With a final blow, her silver sword rams into its heart.

The beast hisses the sound of a million lizards and topples to the floor with a thud. The broken body swirls away into electrified dust particles, sucking up every drop of yellow blood with their exit.

She turns and faces me with the same smile on her face as when she began. A gleam of sweat glistens on her skin.

"Why didn't you chop off its heads?" I ask.

"The beast was a species of the Hydra family. If you sever their heads, they'd grow back, twofold."

I stand and adjust my clothes. "You act like the beast is a real thing." I chuckle, grab a towel hanging on the wall, and toss it to her.

"It is," she says seriously and pats the towel across her forehead. "Don't you have Mythical Studies this year?"

"Yes, but the word mythical implies, um, that it's a myth." I watch her walk to the door. It slides open.

She turns and says, "Yes, mythical." A wry smile touches her face as she adds, "To the Normals."

No
13

DINNER
WITH RAY

WHY DO I FIND IT DIFFICULT BELIEVING IN
mythical animals? I believe in Animates and time travel.
Those two are anomalies in themselves. Our histories claim we
descend from angels, genies, or a million other options, depending on whom you ask. I can believe in mythical creatures too—
right?

I try not to overanalyze the theory. If they're real, I'll have to
let my brain accept it and move on. That's how I deal with my
sci-fantasy life these days.

I rush to my room after watching Ms. Swift fight the two-
headed dragon beast. Not because I'm excited, in fact, I'm very

underwhelmed by what will be taking place this evening—dinner with my dad, Ray.

He's been in Chicago all day on business. He left a message with the office saying that he'd pick me up at six this evening with Aunt Mona. He also requested that I bring my roommates. The fact that he thought of this himself makes me nervous. I wonder if he suspects that Bishop and I are dating.

Even if he's savvy enough to notice that, I decide I won't give him any evidence to latch on to. When Bishop returns to the apartment, I give him strict instructions not to come near me the entire evening. I tell him to pretend I'm his sister, which shouldn't be too difficult since he has one. He doesn't like the idea of hiding our relationship, but I eventually talk him into it—with some persuasive pleading and kissing.

From the moment the elevator of the John Hancock Tower begins its rumble back and forth through the shaft, eventually passing the eightieth floor, I'm convinced that my fear of heights and my life are actually people, and the two are conspiring against me. Together, they play evil tricks daily, figuring out how they can constantly push me into situations where I have to deal with my fear of heights. This is one of those times.

I want to reach for Bishop's hand, to curl up next to him the way I did on the London Eye. Being near him gives me the courage to do what normally seems terrifying. Within fifteen minutes of Ray picking us up, I already want to break my own "no-touching rule" and accept the consequences.

Bishop stands on the opposite side of the compartment in a conversation with Ray, discussing the poetry of Edgar Allan Poe. I knew Bishop would appeal to Ray's intellectual side. They have the love of the written word in common.

My body crams against the wall behind Aunt Mona. I clutch the railing for dear life, breathing in the stagnant air. My ears pop twice, and I almost lose it. I'm okay with a short elevator trip, but one that seems to take ten minutes is out of the question. I'm starting to wonder if I have claustrophobia, too.

The door opens to the ninety-fifth floor, and a whirl of fresh air rushes in. I inhale, pushing past everyone on my way out. Sam starts to make a snide remark, probably about how I'm not a proper lady. Instead, she turns up her nose and glances over at Ray, apparently deciding to hold her tongue.

A man in a suit greets us. He leads us to a reserved dinner table, right next to the window. Bishop pulls out the chair farthest away from the glass, and I quickly sit. This puts me at the head of the table and two seats away from Bishop. He secretly winks at me as everyone settles into his or her seats.

The place is fancy, with lots of glass, too much glass for my taste. The whole city of Chicago opens up before us at the edge of our dinner table, making my stomach queasy.

As the waiter takes our order, I keep pushing on the ground with my foot to make sure that the floor isn't going anywhere. I can't fight the thought that the whole building might tip over, and we'll slide over the edge and into Lake Michigan. I grab a dinner roll from the basket and shove it in my mouth, feeding my anxiety with carbs.

When I'm finally over my fit, I realize that sitting here with everyone just doesn't feel right. Ray isn't a part of my Wandering world, so I don't know what to talk about with him anymore. Right now, he's busy being awed with Sam's long repertoire of extracurricular activities. If Ray requested it, I'm sure she'd jump up to give a rendition of the Sugar Plum Fairy. *Gag.*

Bishop offers me a smile, probably knowing exactly what I'm thinking. I sink into my seat, trying not to smile back.

"So, Sera, excited about the new semester?" Ray asks, and pushes his wire-rimmed glasses farther up his nose.

"Sure, of course, who wouldn't be," I say facetiously and place the napkin in my lap. The waiter walks around, filling our water glasses.

"I just want to tell you how proud I am of you." Ray leans over and slaps me on the back. "The fact that I haven't gotten a call from the principal's office in several months just tells me that it was the right decision to send you to the Academy."

Wow, a compliment. Sort of. I roll my eyes.

"Were you a troublemaker, Sera?" Bishop teases.

"No," I sass. Then I add, "Just misunderstood," under my breath. *And ignored, and undervalued.* I look over at Ray. He's probably thrilled to have me out of his receding dirty-blond hair. Now he can be at his girlfriend's beck and call at all hours of the day.

"I know it's early to ask, but where are you all thinking about going to college?" Ray glances around the table. He's doing his fatherly duty by asking the universally used questions for teenagers.

Sam speaks first, probably because she wants to show off. "I'd like to find myself in New York, splitting my time between Columbia University and the Joffrey School of Ballet." She sits straight in her chair with her shoulders back, gently buttering her bread and sets her utensils down with perfect etiquette.

I snort. Ray flicks his eyes to me and then back to the table at large.

"How about you, Bishop?"

"I'm undecided, sir," he says respectfully. But I know that isn't the case. We've all already discussed going to a wandering university together.

"Sera, where are you thinking of attending?" Sam asks, aiming to put me in the hot seat.

"Um…" I stall as the waiter moves around, placing salad plates on the table. "Well, I was thinking of taking a semester off before college, so I could travel for a few months," I say seriously. That would be my goal if I were a *Normal*.

Ray drops his fork from his mouth. It lands, rattling his salad plate. He drags his napkin across his face, wiping the smile away. He places both elbows on the table; his lips pinch like a fish.

"What?" I ask.

"Seriously, Sera. Why can't you be more focused like Sam, here? She's younger and already knows what she wants."

I flash a look to Sam. She's tilting her head and giving me the *you suck* eyes.

"Well, I think a few months of travel would be a wonderful idea, Sera," Mona chimes in. "It would be an education in itself, Raymond." She attempts to soothe him by rubbing his shoulder.

"Well, we'll see. We'll talk about that later, young lady." He picks up his fork, stabs a piece of lettuce, and tosses it in his mouth, chewing angrily.

The evening is awkward and annoying, especially with Sam aspiring to win the affections of my father. Which isn't very hard to do, considering he would love to have a child just like her. The two are a perfect fit in pretend familyland.

"So, Sera, have any boys caught your eye?" Ray nudges my arm with his. But while I'm choking on my cheesecake, Bishop responds for me.

"Oh, don't be shy, Sera. Don't you fancy that boy, the British chap—the one with the dreamy voice? Isn't that what you called it?" His smile goads.

"Yeah, he's cute, but I don't know," I say, playing along.

"You mean Turner?" Sam asks seriously, looking between us. Bishop and I freeze, shocked that she would dare mention Turner's name.

"Turner? I thought you were dating Bishop?" Mona questions, looking confused.

Ray looks at me and then turns his scorching eyes to Bishop. *Oh, man. This is horrible, like my nightmare come true.* I didn't tell Mona to keep our relationship secret. She's so liberal and hippie that living with your boyfriend in high school probably seems perfectly acceptable to her.

I hide behind my hand, deflating fast.

"No. Actually, Mona, Ray," Bishop says, clearing his throat. "Sera is, in fact, interested in Turner as Sam mentioned." Bishop's lips twist over the words. But he spits them out, for my sake, for his, for whatever will get us out of Ray's crosshairs.

"I know I started this topic," says Ray, "but now it's making me uncomfortable. The thought of you being in a dorm with *boys*—at this age!" Ray shakes his head. "Do we need to have the talk again, Sera?"

That's when my balloon pops, and I die of absolute embarrassment. *My father, asking me if I needed to have "the talk" in front of my friends. My boyfriend!* Someone please, shoot me now.

Sam holds her napkin over her lips, stifling a giggle. Bishop raises his eyebrows and looks out the window, pretending he didn't hear. And Mona, well, she leans toward me over the table, asking if I want her to give me a refresher lecture.

Absolutely humiliated, I push myself away from the table, throw my napkin at Ray, and stalk away from one of my worst evenings ever.

•

Even though I spent most of the weekend avoiding everybody, I'll have to find the strength to make it through the first day of classes. The memory of two nights ago will not leave my mind. I fixate on the expression on Ray's face when he found out I'm dating Bishop. And then the look on Bishop's face when Sam said

I *liked* Turner. Mona tried to make me feel better on the ride home by telling me she had a book I could read if I was too shy for *the talk*.

Mortified, I huddle into my blankets and underneath my pillows. I just want to die.

At least I'm done with Ray's visits for the foreseeable future. At this pace, we'll only reunite every few months. The next torture session won't come until my birthday in November or winter break if I'm lucky.

Something slides under the door. I reluctantly peek out from my pillow cave. A shiny gold envelope sits on the floor.

I groan, toss off the comforter, and roll out of bed. I grab the envelope and run, jumping back onto the mattress, pulling the warmth and protection of the blankets around me.

I rip open the envelope and pull out an invitation. Decorative swirls roll around the border. Pristine calligraphy requests students' presence in the main arcade after lunch today. Obviously Gabe sent this invitation. He's in charge of the school's functions.

I take a quick shower, apply makeup, and then peruse my closet, inspecting my new clothes. New uniforms hang neatly at the front of the closet. They're similar to the year before: a crisp white shirt with little puffy shoulders and a plaid pleated skirt. A hooded cardigan and dark vest hang behind those, allowing two alternating looks. I walk deeper into the closet, eyeing the additions. I run my finger along the edges of the fabric and garment bags then stop on one outfit in particular. The one the *other* me wore the day I saw her in London, crying.

Whatever makes me cry in London is going to happen this year, in this outfit. I pull the hanger out and walk into my room. On tippy toes, I hang the clear garment bag from the closet door. I roll up the plastic bag to take a good look.

Nothing out of the ordinary pops out, a hint to why I'll be crying. I'm not sure why I thought seeing the clothes up close might give a clue. I lift the skirt, inspecting the leggings beneath them and then open the pockets, checking the suede jacket. *Empty.*

I leave the outfit on the door, hanging. I wonder how many times I'll have to wear it before that day in London will come.

I dry my hair, slide on a pair of tights, my new uniform, and a pair of laced ankle boots. When I walk out of my bedroom, Bishop's eyes meet mine. He places a cup of tea and a poetry book on the counter and comes to me, instantly wrapping his long arms around my back. He leans down and brushes his lips to my forehead. I melt into our hug.

"Good morning," he says. "I wasn't sure you would ever leave that room again."

"Thought about it. I just want to forget the other night, if that's okay?"

"What? Are you saying you didn't have a lovely visit with your father?" Sam chimes in, walking into the living room. She grabs the remote and turns on the TV.

"Yeah, it was *great!*" I step away from Bishop and fling myself on the sectional couch.

Gabe's face appears on the TV screen. This is the new thing

this year—a morning show with Academy and Society of Wanderers announcements, hosted by Gabe. He sits behind a desk, dressed in a magenta kimono. His makeup, caked on and powdery white, resembles a Geisha girl.

"Konnichiwa!" Gabe says and folds his hands on the desk. I'd personally be shocked if they stayed there. Gabe doesn't sit still for anything. I suspect not even a morning show.

Bishop relaxes, reaches his arm around my shoulder, and I curl into him.

"It's going to be an exciting year at Washington Square Academy! And by now, you would have received your super-fabulous invitations! This afternoon, I'll be giving you a sneaky peeky of the fall gala which takes place this coming weekend!" Gabe screeches and claps his hands, bouncing in his seat. The cameraman struggles to keep him in the shot.

"Now, on to more serious things." Gabe stiffens, struggling to mimic a real newscaster. "Today, the Society of Wanderers reports an attack on the Washington, D.C., relic archives, one of our largest relic caches. Although no one has claimed responsibility, Grand Master Phineas Levi blames the Underground. He's ordered more security for archive facilities, including schools and universities.

"Tomorrow, Grand Master Levi will lead a meeting of the Society District Senators to discuss the continued malicious efforts of the Underground. He hopes to negotiate peace among all Wanderers and put an end to their rebellious ways."

"Wow, they're actually talking about the Underground? Surprising," I say.

"Yes, well, I think since our encounter last semester, maybe they've decided to be slightly more transparent," Bishop offers.

"School will begin this morning for students in the auditorium in the Tower Building. Mr. Evanston will present the welcome orientation. We ask juniors to stay behind to receive their oath packages." Gabe's composure dissolves, losing its seriousness. He flings his hands around. "Oh—so—exciting! I remember receiving my oath package." He looks far away with nostalgia.

"Oath packages, already?" I say. We're still weeks away from the oath ceremony. I don't really know, just yet, what the packages will include. Thinking about dedicating my life to the Society of Wanderers still doesn't sit well with me.

"It's going to happen, Sera. Get used to it," Sam says and rises in one fluid motion. She seems so much older this year. Of course, she's always been mature, too mature for her age. Instead of being an adult trapped in a child's body, she's now an adult trapped in a teenager's body.

But as annoying as she is, she's right. I should probably start accepting this life. I have no reason to think this existence will be anything less than amazing. Seeing firsthand accounts of history as it unfolds from the everyday to the extraordinary. What Normal wouldn't want what I have? I should just be grateful and embrace who I am.

IN THE AUDITORIUM, WITHIN THE TOWER Building of Olde Town, Headmaster Evanston drones, explaining the mechanics of Wandering. Seniors giggle, gossiping that he repeats the same speech every year. Wanderers, Seers, Protectors, relics, life paths, true time, skipping—he conveniently ignores the fact that we have the extraordinary gift of perfect recall for everything we hear. But I suppose the information is new for the incoming class. I glance around, seeking out the freshly harvested faces.

Bored, my head slowly dips into my palm. The only interesting tidbit he's added thus far is that juniors will be able to wander back as much as two hundred years. Even though I've heard this before, I find the news compelling, wondering where and when our school field trips might lead us this semester.

"Ow!" Sam jabs her elbow into my side, waking me. I rotate my body, attempting to ignore her.

Right before my eyelids sink shut, a distant giggle snaps them open. Over my shoulder, four rows behind, Turner and Perpetua sit in deep conversation. Perpetua stifles a laugh every few moments by covering her mouth with her hand.

When Turner notices my interest, he leans closer to her and whispers. His mouth moves, but I can't decipher the words. This time Perpetua laughs so hard that she doubles over and throws her head between her knees.

The lecture stops.

Mr. Evanston clears his throat. Every student turns to watch Perpetua's body jerking uncontrollably, her face red and tear-streaked with laughter. Turner only shrugs and shakes his head, acting innocent. Mr. Evanston continues his lecture after urging everyone to pay attention.

What can Turner possibly be saying to her that's so funny? And why is he even sitting next to her in the first place? Where are Stuart, her Wanderer, and Jessica, her Seer? I scan the room, finding the two huddled together, looking quite comfy with each other. Maybe they're dating now.

Regardless, seeing Turner and Perpetua together ticks me off. How can he consort with her when he knows she led me off to be killed by Cece? I turn and narrow my eyes. He meets my gaze and smiles, clearly striving to agitate me. He reaches into his vest and pulls out my rosary necklace. It dangles in front of his chest.

He mouths the words, "I win." This instantly angers me. He must have rigged the defense hologram machine so he could watch the fights—our fight! Just remembering how close I came to winning it back—*grrrr!* I want to explode at the thought. There's no end to the ways he'll torture me.

Restless in my seat, I contemplate jumping over four rows of students to tackle him. That's when Bishop places his hand on my knee and clears his throat.

Quickly I turn my attention forward, but I allow my mind to pore over all the ways I'm going to beat Turner's hologram into a messy, electrified pulp. I want that necklace, and I want it now.

•

Three exhausting hours later, the lecture ends. New and senior students are dismissed for their first classes. Headmaster Evanston asks the remaining students to move forward to the seats nearest the stage.

Ms. Midgenet, the Team Tactics instructor, walks up the stairs. When she reaches the top, her short legs shuffle across the floor to a long braided rope hanging from the ceiling. She tugs the cord with all of her weight. Her body dips back, almost hitting the ground. The dark red velvet curtains part, revealing a line of Society soldiers standing at attention behind a long wood table stacked with leather briefcases.

The oath packages.

I squirm in my new seat, feeling uncomfortable. The decision to continue with my secret life as a Wanderer weighs heavily on my conscience. Even though I know I should just accept it, I make a list of the pros and cons in my mind. Bishop and finding my Mom: pros. Everything else: con. The two pros are more than enough to tip the scales, but I can't fight the uncomfortable feeling I have about deciding my whole life right now. I'm not ready on so many levels.

Headmaster Evanston reads out students' names, team by team. He calls Macey's team first. As a group, they rise from their seats and walk ceremoniously to the stage. Each is congratulated for their choice to take the oaths, to become invaluable members of the Society of Wanderers in several weeks. Ms. Midgenet hands them each a briefcase.

Mr. Evanston then calls Perpetua, Stu, and Jessica. Perpetua dances up the stairs and practically pirouettes across the stage. She turns to face the crowd in the spotlight, waving triumphantly. In the blinding light, she still manages to find me in the crowd to taunt me with her victorious gaze. My eyes narrow. She of all people doesn't deserve that case. I mentally stamp her name on my list of cons. The rest of her team accepts their oath packages and exits as the next group approaches.

The headmaster calls our team last. Sam squeezes past, finding the spot in front. Bishop swings his arm, gesturing for me to walk before him. He's always so polite.

Ms. Midgenet hands each of us a briefcase. I grab the handle and the leather box swings to my side. It's heavy, weighty, just like the decision I need to make. I grip the handle tightly. The blood in my fingers rushes away. Mr. Evanston firmly shakes my other hand, extending gratitude for the service I'm going to give to the Society. I nod and smile, then walk across the stage and down the stairs.

Bishop and Sam join the group of huddled juniors. There's a general mood of excitement buzzing through the air. Every student seems happy for this moment, happy to be spending the rest of his or her life in service to the Society. The Society we know so little about even after all this time.

I mill around the outside of the group, concentrating on my pros. That's when I notice Turner. He's still sitting in the back of the auditorium, by himself. No team. No oath package. Not a speck of happiness on his face. He looks at me, and I know he's reading my mind.

I turn away, instantly wanting to hide my feelings. That's when Macey seizes me and throws her long arms around my shoulders. She bubbles over with excitement, gushing loudly about how proud her parents will be, both of them Wanderers.

If Ray knew about my new world, he might be happy, I consider. And my mom, I hope she would be proud, too. So I add these two new possibilities to my list of pros. My mom is proud of me because I'm just like her. The fabricated thought makes me smile with contentment.

Students rush to their rooms to open their packages. But I don't want to know what's inside. I toss the leather briefcase on my bed and then leave the apartment, heading for lunch, happy to leave it behind.

Lunch has a familiar feeling. Macey, Quinn, Xavier, Bishop, Sam, Scarlett, Agnes, and now Atticus Li sit at our lunch table. And to make sure everything plays out properly, Perpetua finds her seat at the table facing me, perfectly positioned so her cold stares can torment me whenever the spirit moves her. Not much has changed since she last stepped foot in this school.

Stu, sitting next to Perpetua, leans around her and waves with his fingertips. Before I can glance away, he blows me a kiss. I don't bother responding. He's as bad as she is, always pushing my buttons.

I focus on the newer person at our table, Atticus Li. He belongs to Scarlett and Agnes as their Protector. Before moving to Chicago, he lived in Vancouver, British Columbia, with his three older sisters. I find it difficult not to stare at his hair. The mohawk, gelled with some kind of cement, makes five perfect points shoot from his scalp. The peaks look as dangerous as knives, and I decide after touching one for myself that they could easily kill someone in a dark alley. Even with his deadly hair, his almond eyes and smile are very warm and friendly. Right now, he and Bishop are discussing the fighting technique, capoeira.

We eat and Macey gabs about her family trip to Australia. Agnes and Atticus talk about a date they went on to a Frank Sinatra concert in 1958, in Monte Carlo. And Sam instructs me on proper table manners by pushing my elbows off the table and suggesting that I cross my legs at my ankles and not my knee.

I avoid all discussions related to the oath package. The words I do hear from others: cell phone, unlimited credit card, Society uniform—these items scare me.

•

After lunch, students crowd the second floor balconies, looking down into the main atrium. I lean against the thick marble railing, letting my gaze drift around the room, taking note of the new faces. I can imagine the confusion they must feel. They'll be wondering how they took a nosedive into the Wandering Academy. The thought makes me feel sorry for them, but happy that I'm well past the point of struggling to make myself believe every unbelievable thing that's shoved down my throat.

Society soldiers roam the room with authority. They carry no weapons, even though they were sent to protect us from possible attacks by the Underground. I can't help wondering what the likelihood of that really is. What could they possibly want with anything here?

One guard points toward the ceiling. That's when I look up and see Turner. He dangles from a wire at the very top of the atrium. He's installing some kind of machine. It makes me uneasy seeing him there. It doesn't look safe, but nothing that involves a person hanging sixty feet in midair seems safe to me.

"Turner, are we ready?" Professor Raunnebaum yells to him from the first floor. Even though the two are separated by five floors, the words echo around the entire atrium. Every student looks up, noticing him too.

"It's ready!" Turner yells down to the professor, giving him a thumbs-up. That's when Turner pushes off the wall with his feet, swaying on his wire. He pushes back and forth slowly, gaining height like a child's swing. When he's gained enough momentum, he unlatches his safety, releasing himself from the wire and flies through the air onto a nearby balcony. Every single student gasps in unison at his dangerous stunt. He safely appears from behind the wall and several students applaud.

Even though his idiocy alarms me, I'm a little envious of his fearlessness.

A cranking noise fills the atrium. Everyone jolts, looking for the source. Black metal sleeves slide over every window. They slam shut and a hundred locks click simultaneously with an ominous sound. Silence races through the room. I never knew that the school could go into complete lockdown and, I suspect, neither did anyone else.

I can't see anything in the stygian blackness. Bishop grabs my hand and pulls me closer. From the shuffling that transpires, other Protectors are probably doing the same.

"What's going on?" Sam whispers.

Nº
15
A Preview

"I'M SURE IT'S JUST GABE'S THEATRICS, BUT STAY close, just in case," Bishop says.

Just as a chaotic rumble of nervousness breaks through the crowd, something strange starts to happen. Beautiful little twinkling notes from a pipe organ fill the entire room. The sound is eerie, magical, and beautiful, all at the same time. The music resonates through my body, causing the hair on my arms to rise away from my skin.

From the ceiling, a hazy, undulating, electrified dust solidifies into one hundred ornate parasols. Holographic woman in festive Victorian corsets, short ruffled skirts, and fishnet stockings hang below each of them like a troupe of glowing Mary Poppins. All of them float, descending slowly through the room at various heights, as the organ music continues.

The crowd coos.

When the ladies land, they run to gather in a group. Huddling together with their parasols above them, they form a beautiful solid mass. And that's when the music quickens. The women spin their parasols as the music crescendos into a climax. Snapping their umbrellas shut, they dramatically fall away to the ground, revealing Gabe standing at the center.

"Come one, come all, to Gabe's extraordinary vaudeville circus!" he announces theatrically. The crowd roars. Now in his element, Gabe smiles brightly. Somehow the smell of popcorn and warm salty peanuts wafts through the space, making my mouth water.

"And no circus would be complete without a *ringleader!*" he yells and bows, taking off his sparkling miniature top hat. With a flick of his wrist, he tosses it, sending it spiraling into the crowd. Students roar louder.

To a dance song remixed with organ circus music, Gabe sashays in a circle. He slides his white-gloved hands over his fanciful corset with long tails extending down the back of his legs and onto the floor. His palms slide onto his tuxedo pants and up to a lacy white collar. It stands on end like a fan behind his neck, looking like an Elizabethan ruff.

"We've got a sneaky-peeky of the fall gala dance that will blow your little pumpkin-headed minds!" Confetti shoots from his hands. Sparkles flutter through the air.

A holographic elephant walks into the arcade, seemingly out of a solid wall. The elephant, decorated in cascades of red velvet and fancy gold trim, bows to one knee, extending its trunk. Gabe steps up and perches himself on the elephant's head. The massive animal turns slowly, allowing Gabe to blow kisses to the crowd.

"What would a circus be without *these?*" Gabe points across the room. A spotlight pops on. Acrobats rush out of the brilliant light, down the steps, and flip themselves over the backside of the elephant. They twirl through the air, twisting their bodies like tornados.

"And what about *these?*" Gabe yells with excitement and points dramatically in a new direction. A spotlight pops on revealing jugglers. The men, dressed like mimes, toss flaming clubs toward the ceiling. Fireballs float through the air for an impossible length of time before they race back down to their owners. Even though I know they're holograms, I lean away from the railing every time one streams past, because I'm certain I feel the heat of the flames on my face.

Monster-sized holographic lions roar and saunter down the main stairs, weaving in and around students toward our group. Their paws are so large, they barely fit in the width of a single step. Sam edges behind me, ducking.

A holographic vaudeville circus has broken out before our eyes. Except for a hazing electrical zap here and there, every holographic performer, animal, and fanciful costume appears as real as the people standing next to me. Professor Raunnebaum is an inventive genius and Gabe is a theatrical one.

When the sideshow acts multiply into an absolute frenzy, the holograms snap off. After a dramatic moment, a single spotlight pops on. Gabe stands alone, center stage, in a new outfit. Red and orange sequined flames wrap around the legs of his white jumpsuit. A scarlet cape blows behind him, making him look like a glamorous Elvis impersonator.

Gabe stands, statue still, chin lifted dramatically, hands clenched at hips and legs slightly spread, solid with authority. He rises from the floor as though he's standing on a platform. But as he drifts higher into the air, he seems to be standing on top of a holographic smoke stack. When the stack's height reaches the fourth floor, Gabe hops up in the air, snapping his legs and arms close to his body. He falls straight down the smokestack pipe, disappearing. The pipe crashes, falling to one side, revealing its true purpose. With a blast of smoke and a loud *kaboom* that makes everyone cover their ears, Gabe shoots out of the cannon, arcing through the air and over our heads. A cloud of iridescent smoke follows him.

"Prepare to be amazed!" he yells, right before he dissipates into a ring of shimmering wander dust. Confetti pours from the ceiling, raining down. The lights snap off again, leaving us in complete darkness.

Everyone cheers and whistles, delighted by the extravaganza, one that ended with a literal bang. I wonder how Gabe will top the experience at the actual gala. But it's stupid for me to think that he won't.

The holograms and their realism shock everyone. Even I'm excited by the thought of what they can do, how they interact seamlessly with the real world. Like those I use in my defense training, these are called touchable holograms. Scientifically, they are light years beyond what the Normals now know as holograms. This is the machine that Turner was installing on the ceiling—the projectors that make the solid 3-D images come to life.

When the metal shades retract from the windows, revealing the outside sunlight, students migrate downstairs into Olde Town, toward their next class. My next class is the Physics of Wandering with Professor Raunnebaum.

Sam, Bishop, and I walk across the bridge, through the Lion's Gate. We step into the far tunnel, weaving underneath the West Academy and past the Relic Archives entrance. Several hundred paces in, the lanterns for the Archive Library entrance flicker to life. We push through the tall doors and into the room. Several students follow.

The library, wrapped in mahogany bookshelves lined with antiquated books, rises several stories high. Every time I enter this room, a musty vanilla aroma tickles my nose. A catwalk winds around the second and third floors. A brass chandelier hangs, centered, from the ceiling. The room's architecture is familiar, duplicated over and over again in connecting chambers. How many times, I can't be sure.

Professor Raunnebaum stands at the front of the main room, tinkering with a contraption sitting on his desk. He peers up from over his glasses when we walk in.

"Come in! Come in! Take a seat, and I'll be with you in one moment." He gestures toward the long desks before him. Bishop, Sam, and I sit in the second row. I slide into the aisle seat and lean back in my chair.

I'm busy absorbing the room when a finger slowly slides across the width of my desktop. My eyes follow the arm attached. Perpetua flashes a fake smile and tosses her body into the seat right in front of mine. She crosses her bare legs at the knee. Her skirt, rolled at the waist, makes the length ten inches shorter than mine. I guess the more leg she shows, the more attention she commands from the boys. She swings her arm over the back of the chair and turns.

"Did you find my crystal yet, witch?" she asks.

"Really? Still crying about your mysterious rock?" I laugh a little, knowing it will annoy her.

"Perpetua, I told you, she doesn't know anything about it," Bishop offers. But when I look at him, it seems as though he knows more about this than me.

"Maybe she doesn't have it—*yet*," she says to Bishop, then turns to give me a cold stare. "But when you *do* take it," she leans onto my desk, moving right up to my face, "know that there will be hell to pay."

"Okay, class!" Professor Raunnebaum claps his hands twice. "Let's get started, shall we?"

Perpetua turns around and smiles at the teacher, folding her hands on her desk. Her ponytail bobs gently behind her. In my mind, I imagine leaning over and ripping it off her head.

I take out a pen and paper, not for taking notes, but for passing notes. On the small pad, I scribble, "What do you know about her crystal?" I tilt the note toward Bishop.

He only shrugs, whispering, "Nothing."

I study his face. I want to believe him, but I can't, only because he seems so unconcerned about it. Sure, he rescued me from her beat-down in the hall the other day, but why isn't he concerned beyond that? Especially when she's still pushing the idea that I somehow have this stupid rock of hers—something I haven't taken *yet*. Resolving the issue quickly is something he would have done in the past.

I analyze the situation until Professor Raunnebaum starts the lecture.

"This is going to be a very exciting class, indeed," the professor says as he paces, staring intently at the floor. "We'll be discussing general relativity, the speed of light, wormholes, paradoxes, entanglement, and many other scientific theories. All things you may have heard about, but we'll be analyzing them from a new point of view. One that you may not be familiar with, a Wanderer's point of view!" His arms jerk, swinging in choppy movements.

He turns to face the class and quickly glances around before he races through his words again. "Galileo Galilei,

Sir Isaac Newton, Albert Einstein—geniuses, yes! But they lacked knowledge of one thing—one thing that would change their entire perspective of time travel. And what is that?" He stops, snapping his legs closed, staring at no one in particular.

Sam's arm pops up, extending rigid above her head.

"Yes, Miss James." The professor nods, his tangled hair jolts.

"Us. They have no knowledge of Wanderers."

"Exactly!" The professor holds up his finger, pointing into the air with a plastic smile. "So, we'll start with what the Normals theorize to be true, then we'll add in the missing details!" He runs toward the contraption he's been tinkering with, picks it up, and runs to the back of the class.

The library lights click off. The machine snaps on.

"I'll have you enjoy a lecture from Mr. Albert Einstein, himself. A filmed lecture given in the 1920s at Princeton University on the Theory of Relativity," he says with excitement.

A hologram buzzes in and out, sputtering blue electrical charges. The figure walks around the front of the class before its form completely solidifies. The man bears small resemblance to the Albert Einstein I've seen in photos. This man is much younger; the only similarity is his thick black mustache. He brushes his hand over his coarse salt-and-pepper hair and begins speaking with a heavy German accent.

No
16

HISTORY &
MYTHOLOGY

WHEN WE ARRIVE FOR OUR NEXT CLASS, Wandering Histories and Mythologies, Mr. Attah Tash sits with his long dark legs crossed on a small, ornately carved pedestal, meditating. His hands rest, palm up, two fingertips touching. Three relics float at eye level before him. Together, the objects blaze, shimmering and sparkling.

Sam sits at the very front; her insightful eyes evaluate the small Indian man with thick black hair and a wide brow line. Surely she's admiring his phenomenal abilities. The more experienced the Seer, the brighter a relic burns.

Students quietly sit on silk pillows scattered around the tiled floor. Bishop and I settle at the back of the intimate room. The space reminds me of the Moroccan restaurant he took me to in London. Just like he did that night on several occasions, he grabs my hand and plants a kiss on my palm. He gazes intently into my eyes, and I realize he's thinking the same thing, which makes me smile.

When the class bell rings, Mr. Tash inhales an enormous breath, making his chest rise. His dark eyes flutter open, and he smiles. Even as he relaxes his meditative stance, the relics, which I can now see are pieces of chalk, continue their playful levitation, orbiting around his head like planets.

"Welcome, class," he says, but continues to hold his pose.

"Whoa!" The class gasps in unison at the aged Seer's control. I've heard rumors that well-developed Seers can control objects with levitation even in their waking states like telekinesis, but I've never seen it for myself.

One piece of chalk glides away from his body and lands, poised to write on the chalkboard. With only air to hold it up, it scratches the word, Gibeon, in capital letters across the surface.

"Washington, D.C., London, Paris, Bangkok, New Delhi—every state or country has its own capital. Gibeon is the Society of Wanderers' capital," Mr. Tash says, his voice rich with an Indian accent. "Some of you may have heard about it, but soon, as new members of the Society, you will make a pilgrimage there yourselves. This is one of the cities of a time. A place where your entire team can travel together."

This information induces a cheer from the class.

"Yes, very exciting, indeed," he agrees.

Mr. Tash walks to the edge of the chalkboard, where he positions himself into a new yoga pose. His hands rest palm to palm, and he raises them above his head, pointing skyward. Then he lifts one foot, anchoring it on his opposing thigh like a flamingo. "Please, class, stand and try the tree pose with me. A balanced and quiet mind is a disciplined one."

Sam easily arranges herself in the awkward pose. Somehow, when I try, I'm leaning on Bishop, using him as a crutch. There are quick giggles around the room. Students bobble and fall over, then try the pose again.

Mr. Tash releases his stance and walks around to instruct each member.

"Seraphina, you must use your core, hold your stomach strong, and rely on yourself to keep this pose, not Mr. Bishop." He gently straightens my body, pulling me away from Bishop. "Breathe as though meditating." He demonstrates the proper technique.

I manage to hold the pose, which makes Mr. Tash smile. Though, while I should be concentrating, I can only think of how glad I am that Macey isn't here. We'd collapse to the floor in laughter over a history class taught in conjunction with yoga.

"Yes, wonderful! You've got it! This will increase everyone's strength, flexibility, and alignment," Mr. Tash praises in a gentle voice.

"Gibeon's the only place where time literally stands still. At any moment in history, no person knows the true position of

Gibeon. Its secret location on earth randomly switches, never allowing it to latch on to any time zone."

"How does an entire city move locations?" I ask. My pose wavers, and I lose my balance. My toes touch the ground. Quickly, I reestablish myself as a yoga tree.

"The relocation of the city is random and quite violent. Great forces of nature such as earthquakes, volcanic eruptions, hurricanes, and tsunamis often mask the geological shift," he explains.

"The Grand Lodge, the capitol building, is where your oaths to the Society will take place." He walks to the front of the class. The second piece of chalk leaves from circling his head and draws a detailed picture on the board.

"This," Mr. Tash points to the new drawing, "is the Grand Lodge. It's the most important building in the city of Gibeon, and it's where governing decisions are made on behalf of the Society."

The drawing is that of a ziggurat, a steeply pitched, stair-stepped building reminiscent of the ancient flat-topped pyramid-like temples in Chichen-Itza, Saqqara, and many other places throughout the world.

"As you can see here, Animates patrol every level of the building. They keep a watchful eye over the city and its numerous inhabitants, promoting balance and harmony among our kind."

"Now, class, release your tree pose and please move to a high lunge." Mr. Tash starts with his feet together, hands in a prayer, then he lunges backward, deepening himself into the pose, completely in control.

I rearrange my body into the easier pose. Out of the corner of my eye, I see Bishop teeter, almost losing his balance completely. I smile but try to remain focused.

"The history of Gibeon is a complicated one. The city itself was a gift from our Makers as a place for our kind to colonize on earth.

"At that time, the city of Gibeon did not move. For a thousand years, Wanderers lived happily in Gibeon. But it's said that a young woman roamed past the limits of the city and befriended those of a nearby village of Normals. Although forbidden by our Makers, she taught the Normals our secrets: magic, weaponry, science, mathematics, farming, hunting, etc., giving them the keys to better themselves, and perhaps, become more evolved than was meant to be. She also fell in love with a Normal.

"This secretly continued for some time until the nearby town, whose rulers had become corrupt, drunk on their new knowledge acquired from the young girl, decided to attack Gibeon for its wealth of unlimited enlightenment.

"Gibeon, always peaceful, was suddenly occupied by Normals.

"The Makers immediately wiped out the new rulers and punished Gibeon's inhabitants for the girl's actions. Each was stripped of their powers—their wings, their magic, and their super-strength, whatever non-human power they possessed. But they bestowed on us a new ability—Wandering—so that we could time travel and always look back and learn from our mistakes. The Makers hoped that Wanderers would endeavor to become more evolved. And in dividing the ability between three persons—Wanderer, Seer, and Protector—each would have to consider their actions from many points of view.

"As further punishment, the Makers put Gibeon in motion, never allowing it to rest and move through time normally. So randomly, sometimes several times a day, the city moves violently as a reminder of their shortcomings and so that Normals would not find their location ever again.

"Of course, this is mythology. There are many different stories of our beginnings. Some Wanderers believe and some do not. Since then, Wanderers have left the limits of Gibeon, and mingled with Normals quite seamlessly. In doing so, many Wanderers have accepted the ways, religions, and customs of the Normals."

"The city moving daily must lend some truth to the story," Bishop remarks.

"Yes, Mr. Bishop, I completely agree. There are many truths to learn from our mythology," says Mr. Tash with a wide smile.

"With your new wandering compasses from your oath package, you can travel to Gibeon. But please, when you finally make your pilgrimage, do not be shocked by the people visiting from various time periods. During my recent visit, I chatted with Jules Verne. Very exciting, indeed."

This comment launches a new peppering of questions. Several minutes pass before Mr. Tash returns to his lecture.

"Now, please take out your wandering compasses," Mr. Tash instructs.

I have yet to open my oath package, so I drag myself closer to Bishop. From his vest pocket, he pulls out a clear glass orb with a compass suspended in the middle. It hangs from a looped leather band, one that can easily fit around his wrist. The leather is decorated, embossed with the markings of a Protector, a scorpion. When I lean in to admire the compass' face, I notice that the name, Gibeon, sits in the place of a north marker. Several names of other wandering cities are marked around the edges. These must be the other cities of time.

"I will teach you how to use these now." Mr. Tash steps to the center of the room.

Students stack pillows at the wall and stand in a circle surrounding Mr. Tash.

"Pay close attention, class, to everything that I do. The compass can be used to travel back and forth from Gibeon. You cannot wander there normally because a life path cannot be connected with a location that moves, but you may wander normally from Gibeon, back home, if necessary."

Mr. Tash stands with one bare foot in front of the other. His hand, positioned at his hip, holds the leather strap loosely around his wrist, compass tucked into his cupped fingers. With a quick flick of his hand, a bronze chain unwinds from around the compass like a yoyo, dropping the orb toward the floor.

"Keep the name *Gibeon* in your head as your keyword," he reminds.

Mr. Tash rocks forward and back, changing his weight from one foot to the other. Near the floor, the compass moves with him, swinging like a pendulum. He flicks his wrist again, quicker this time, and the compass rotates in a complete circle at the end of the chain. The orb whirls in wide rotations repeatedly, building speed and creating a whipping sound, which intensifies into a wild buzz.

Mr. Tash's body blurs, disconnecting with true time. And after a few seconds, he's completely gone—vanished to Gibeon.

We stare at each other in shock. For me, it's the first time I've seen someone wander without the aid of falling or running—the world, for once, not crashing, catapulting them into a wormhole.

Amazing.

A blur reappears, accompanied by the buzzing whirl of the compass. Mr. Tash's body solidifies. While lost in my astonishment, the bell rings, signaling the end of class.

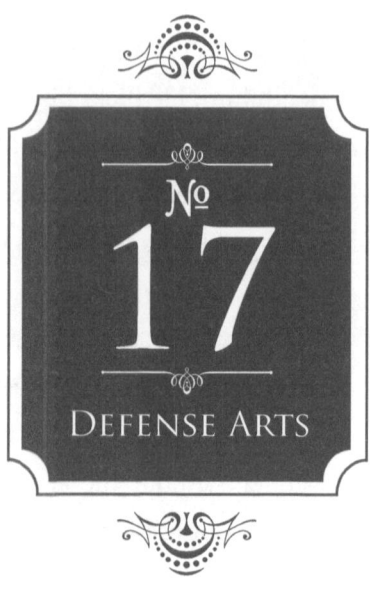

No

17

DEFENSE ARTS

I'M IN THE CLASS I'D BEEN DREADING ALL summer, Defense Arts. Not because I don't want to improve. Of course, I do, but I'm still not ready to reveal my improved abilities to Bishop. He'll not only be hurt but he'll easily figure out my plan—to go back and save my mom. That's something I must do alone.

After changing into workout uniforms, a small group of students meets in the Defense Arts gymnasium. The person I really wish wasn't here stands nearby, peering at her reflection in the mirrored wall, primping.

I look away from Perpetua, only to see another person I dislike.

"*Hello*, Sera." Stu strolls over with his lanky, awkward walk. "You're looking as lovely as ever, if you don't mind me saying so." He grabs his pockets, adjusting his pants. I instantly feel dirty, standing near him. His personality oozes an off-putting, slimy confidence.

"Actually, *I* mind," says Bishop. He stands over us and crosses his arms, giving Stu a stern look.

"Whoa." Stu holds up his palms in defense. "Hey, man. Just came over to say hi." He retreats with false remorse, then quickly regains his overconfident swagger.

"Thanks for saving me." I turn to Bishop.

"That's what I'm here for," he says and smiles.

"It just makes me angry to know that they're back," I complain. Bishop rubs the length of my arms. "Why would they do something like that? Does Terease *really* think they're not a threat anymore?"

"No, I doubt it. But in this case, the Society made a trade for something they need, info on Cece's whereabouts."

"Have they even looked for her yet?" I've held out hope that I'll hear about a raid on the Underground before it takes place. In my mind, I imagine sneaking out to join the raiding group—that, or eventually using the rosary to find my mom. Whichever comes first, it doesn't matter. The result will be the same.

"Not as far as I know, but I'll keep my ears open. I know *I'll* sleep better when they aren't a threat to you anymore," Bishop says. "But not that it matters, Sera, I'll never let anyone like that near you again." He slides his finger under my chin to raise my lips level with his. He gives me the smallest, sweetest kiss.

"I guess," I grumble, trying not to smile. His kisses disarm me. Even still, I really need to get the rosary necklace back from Turner. It would be nice to find my mom and never have to think about Cece and the Underground ever again. My next thought: contemplating how to sneak out of the apartment tonight, so I can square off with Hologram Turner. He will lose eventually.

"We'll start today's class with warm-ups. Then we'll practice one-on-one combat," announces Ms. Swift as she walks into the middle of the room. "Now everyone go ahead and spread out." She directs us with her arms until we stand at an acceptable distance from one another.

She then drops to the floor, leading everyone through a prescribed stretching routine, advising us to do so before every class. She explains this will lengthen our muscles, warm them up, and help reduce injury.

"Now, I want everyone to partner with someone *not* on your team," Ms. Swift says. I look around awkwardly, wishing Macey were here. Instead, I find Scarlett, the Seer who sits with our group at lunch.

With the help of Atticus Li, Ms. Swift demonstrates protecting yourself from an attacker who grabs you from behind. Atticus attacks Ms. Swift, throwing his arms around her neck. She twists, securing herself to his shoulder, then flips him over. He moans, lying on the floor in front of her. She hovers in a defensive crouched position. When she determines he's down for good, she pops up with her hands on her hips.

Together, she and Atticus show the class two additional defensive moves.

"Now, try all three moves with your partner. Take turns playing the attacker," Ms. Swift suggests.

I turn to Scarlett, feeling a little guilty about fighting the pixie-like girl. She doesn't seem a bit nervous as she dances into position behind me.

"Ready?" she asks in a cheerful voice.

"Go," I say, quickly trying to decide how hard I should be. *Go easy.*

I don't even hear her running, but I know she's coming. The hair on my arms stands on end. Something within me senses the danger. She jumps, grasping my back. Her arms and legs wrap around my body like a binding rope. Twisting my torso, I flip her. But when she doesn't let go, I flop on top of her with a thud.

She moans.

I quickly jump up. "Are you okay?" I stretch out a hand to help her stand.

"You're really strong. You almost yanked my arms out of the sockets." She rubs her shoulders then rotates them like wings.

I wince. "Sorry." I thought I was being careful.

We move on to the other moves. More gingerly this time,

I dance around her, letting her win every time.

"Are you feeling okay?" Ms. Swift pats my shoulder in between matches.

"Yeah, why?" She looks at me as though she knows I can do better—much better.

She turns to the class. "All right, let's switch partners."

But this time, Ms. Swift rearranges the groups. Scarlett stands in front of Stu, and I, in front of Perpetua. Poor Scarlett; I cringe at her match-up. She looks over, pushes a blonde tress behind her ear, and gives me a worried smile.

She probably feels sorry for me, too. My feelings for Perpetua aren't exactly a secret. I look over at Perpetua. She paces the floor, glaring at me.

Ms. Swift stands in the center of the room with her arms crossed over her gray jumpsuit. "All right, everyone. Try the routine again with your new partner."

Perpetua looks over and gives me one of her evil little smiles. Maybe I can pulverize her while no one's watching.

"I'll attack first," she says and settles into position.

My eyes quickly sweep the room. Every student, including Bishop, is focused on his or her match. It can't hurt, just this once. I wrangle a smile.

The feeling of danger hits faster this time. Perpetua's grip rips around my throat. As a Protector, her skills are far superior to Scarlett's.

To confuse her, I deviate from the lesson. I grab her arm and twist to face her. I lift my knee to her stomach but in a blurred streak, she twists out of my grasp. Kick. Knee. Punch. Turn. Sweep. Flip. The motions repeat with the force of an earthquake. We're locked in an even match until I consider what her weakness might be. I position myself for the final attack; one I know will end this.

Out of the corner of my eye, I see Bishop stop to watch our match. And in that instant, I allow Perpetua to control the fight. After a few quick, painful movements, she victoriously stands over me, twisting my arm into submission and smashing my face into the mat with her foot.

"Okay, class. That's enough for today." Ms. Swift blows her whistle.

Perpetua gives my arm one last jerk for good measure, then thrusts it away. My numb limb falls lifelessly to the ground. She steps over my body and struts away, leaving with an air of superiority. Stu blows me a secret kiss before he and Jessica leave the classroom arm in arm.

"Are you all right?" Bishop rushes to my rescue and lifts me.

"If you didn't aggravate Perpetua, maybe she'd leave you alone," Sam lectures, standing with her arms crossed, shaking her head.

I give her a dirty look. Does she really think that being nice to Perpetua will make a difference?

"I saw the way you prodded her in Physics," she continues.

"I'm not the one who's delusional, Sam. She thinks I stole some stupid crystal of hers."

"Ms. Swift, I think you should have stopped the match. You shouldn't have paired Sera with Perpetua. Sera didn't have a chance," Bishop explains to Ms. Swift when she approaches.

I lean my head into Bishop's shoulder and cling to his waist. Having my butt kicked is worth the price of allowing Bishop to feel like he still needs to protect me.

Ms. Swift only glances between Bishop and me with a quizzical expression. But when she doesn't respond to his complaint, an anxious flutter surges through my body. I hope she won't contradict him and explain why she thinks I can handle Perpetua. I'm sure Professor Raunnebaum has filled her in on my extracurricular activities.

"Ah, Sera—why don't you stay and chat for a moment?" Ms. Swift asks.

"Will you be okay?" Bishop tilts my face up toward his and searches my eyes.

"Of course," I say, still acting fragile. Nervousness flutters through my body. I lift on my tiptoes and give him a kiss on the cheek. "I'll see you at the apartment."

Bishop and Sam leave, and I turn to Ms. Swift.

"Sera, why don't you tell me why you let Perpetua win?" She walks to the rack of weapons and selects a machete from the wall.

"I don't know what you mean," I lie.

"I think you do." She strolls to the middle of the room, twirling the large knife. The blade flashes every time it catches the light.

"There's no reason I can think of for you to throw a fight." The machete flips, whirling in the air. She catches the hilt and begins to pace.

"Why would you think I could beat a Protector? I'm just a Wand—"

Ms. Swift hurls the machete. It flies across the room, racing toward my face.

Nº
18
CLOSING IN

WITHOUT REALIZING IT, I LIFT MY HANDS to stop the machete. When I comprehend what I've done, the blade sits an inch from my nose, its death trail halted between the palms of my hands. I caught it. *I caught the freakin' thing!* My eyes bulge, and I release the knife from shock. It drops to the floor in front of my feet with a loud clank.

"Are you out of your mind?" I scream. My heart races.

Ms. Swift walks forward and nonchalantly snatches the blade from the floor and twirls it again.

"What's wrong with you?"

"I expect you to come to the next class ready to show

me your *full* potential, Miss Parrish." She tosses the machete into the air again. Her movements are so fast, it appears as though there are three knives instead of one. "Do I make myself clear?" She fixes me with a pointed stare.

Trembling, I nod my head and dart for the door before she can test whether I can save myself from being split in half by a machete a second time.

I run out of the training room, through the gymnasium, and into the pitch-black tunnel toward Olde Town. *Is she out of her mind?* How did she know that I could even catch that thing? I could have died! My stomach churns, remembering the shining blade and my horrified eyes reflecting back at me.

Turner's silhouette appears in the light at the end of the tunnel. "What's wrong?" he asks, assessing my fearful face.

I don't answer, I just keep moving. When I race past him, he grabs my arm and spins me back to face him.

"What's going on, Sera?"

"Nothing!" I yank my arm away and keep walking. He follows as I stomp across the courtyard. Students turn to watch. I look around at their curious faces, and then my eyes meet Bishop's. He stands at the raptor entrance gate with a furious look on his face. His fists drop to his side, and he races forward.

"What did you do to her?" he yells across the courtyard, pointing at Turner. His jaw clenches. Anger visibly pulses through his body, turning his face red with emotion.

"He didn't do anything, Bishop." I rush to him, pushing

my palms into his chest to hold him back.

"What's going on, then?" He looks at me and back at Turner. "I can see you're upset. I sensed fear in your emotions all the way across the building."

"It's nothing." I look at Turner who stares at me with his arms crossed, his mouth forced into a line. Bishop struggles to get around me, but I push back even harder. Another fight between the two will only make things worse.

"What do we have here?" Terease appears. She glides between us, sucking in the tension like perfumed-laced air as it swirls around her face.

Bishop stiffens, drops his arms over my shoulder, and pulls me closer.

"It's nothing, Terease," I offer in the calmest voice I can muster.

"A misunderstanding," Turner suggests casually.

Terease flings her silky black bob around and faces Bishop. "Is this true, Bishop?" She crosses her arms.

His body tightens into a statue. He stares at Turner with revulsion. "A misunderstanding," Bishop finally repeats through grinding teeth.

I relax when he says the words, knowing there's no reason for Terease to reprimand us.

"Fine," Terease relents, her red lips twist over the words. I can tell she hoped for a confrontation. For some reason, she enjoys the hostility between them. "I'll be watching." She shoots us a warning with her horrid obsidian eyes. We look away, not wanting to invite her into our minds.

"Go!" she screams.

The city, filled with students, has come to a complete halt to silently watch the turbulent exchange.

Bishop and I turn to leave. When I glance back over my shoulder, Turner stands next to the obelisk with his arms crossed, staring at me.

I rush into the apartment, stomping toward my bedroom. "Hold on, Sera," Bishop requests.

"I already told you, *Max*, nothing happened!" I explode, using his first name because I know he hates it. He's made me so angry, I can't help it. The entire walk to the apartment consisted of Bishop attempting to coerce me into telling him that Turner did something to me. It's as though he wants it to be true, a reason to hate his brother.

Of course, my life would be made a million times easier if I could just tell Bishop the truth. *Ms. Swift almost killed me with a machete. But she didn't, because somehow, I saved myself. She knew I would. I'm a better fighter than you realize and possibly better than you.* But that information will hurt him, and I can't tell him yet. Can I tell him before Miss Swift's next class on Friday? What will she do if I don't practice to my full potential?

"Sera, I'm sorry." I turn to face him before I open my bedroom door. He walks across the room with his arms open. "I made a mistake. If you say that Turner had nothing to do with upsetting you, then I believe you." He rubs the length of my arms and searches my eyes for an acceptance of his apology.

"I promise," I say. "He had nothing to do with anything."

"I believe you." He leans in and wraps his long arms around my waist. "If there's anything you want to talk about, I'll be in my room." He holds me at arm's length. "Okay?"

"I think I just want to be alone for a little while. I'll meet you and Sam for dinner later." I look around his shoulder. Sam peeks out of her bedroom door, assessing the situation. She shakes her head and retreats without saying a word.

I disappear into my room and lean my back against the closed door, letting out a long exhale. Bishop hesitates on the other side, but finally, his footsteps move away.

The long day, filled with so much drama, exhausts me. I drop onto my bed and let out a dramatic moan. I burrow into my pillow, then kick off my shoes and curl into a fetal position.

I want to rest, but I can't. My oath package sits nearby, taunting me to look inside.

Well-worn leather encases the ancient-looking box. Gold rivets line the edges. A shining Society of Wanderers crest spreads across the front. A ribbon of Latin text reading *Tempus Rerum Imperator* floats above a gold obelisk, the sun, and its shining beams of light. A handless clock encircles the scene. I run my hands over the miniature gilt relief, taking the time to trace the edges of each rivet with my fingertip.

I stare at the box for at least an hour before I finally open it. I place my thumb on the recognition pad. The latch releases with the touch of my finger, and then I lift the top. The hinges lock open and into place.

There are many items inside, but the one I zero in on immediately is a cell phone. I haven't owned one since I lost mine when I moved to Chicago. My *other self* used this phone in London, the day I wandered to see Bishop over the summer. I'm certain.

As items from that day in London appear in my life—the outfit and the cell phone—I sense something closing in. But what it means, I'm not sure. I toss the phone into the box.

Next, I pick up the neatly folded uniform. Holding it at a distance, I get a better look. The military-style suit is a fitted gray jacket with black piping, leather shoulder pads, and a metal emblem on the upper arm. Gray slacks, a black hooded cloak, and a pair of steel-toe boots rest inside the case. Obviously I'm expected to wear this on the day of oaths. The thought makes me nervous.

I pick up the Society of Wanderers handbook and quickly flip through. Whatever it says, I don't care. I drop it into the box and move on to the next item, a shiny gold credit card.

My name is embossed in silver letters. When tilting the prismatic reflective surface perfectly with the light, my face appears in 3-D, hovering above the card. Through gossip, I've heard the credit card has no spending limit. As unsettling as this is, my mind immediately drifts to a pair of spiky heels I admired in a downtown store window. Knowing Gabe, they're probably already in my new wardrobe. I just have to get on the floor in the closet and look.

The last item is my Wandering compass. The leather strap is unique, embossed with the symbol of a Wanderer—feathered wings.

I reach to close the top of the package, then stop. Instead, I lean in closer to look at a miniature oil painting mounted on the inside of the box within an ornate Victorian frame. Cracks spread along the surface, but their deep grooves don't mar the beauty of the painting. In puffy clouds, angels swoop from the sky, standing on silver disks. An obelisk sits to one side in front of a beaming sun. Figures on the ground look as though they're running. Running to wander, I suppose. I squint, looking to see their faces, but time has worn their expressions away.

The announcement for dinner pulls me out of the painting. I roll out of bed and head for the mirror, pinch my cheeks, and then pull my hair into one low braid. In the closet, I find an outfit to wear, something nice enough for dinner, but also comfortable enough to secretly fight Hologram Turner later.

When I walk out of the apartment, Bishop and Sam have already left. In the hall, some students are overloaded with shopping bags, rushing to their apartments from outings with their shiny new credit cards. Excitement, much like that of Christmas, buzzes through the school. The scene is no different when I reach the dining room.

Quinn waves as he zooms past on a brand new long-board skateboard. Scarlett and Agnes appear with matching haircuts, dyed light pink. One hairdo is cropped with spikes; the other is rolled in soft curls like a 1940s pinup girl. Perpetua walks ahead in a new slutty outfit and the same spiky heels I had been dreaming about. Annoyed, I hang back until she takes her normal seat. Then I dart for mine.

"Check it out." Macey holds up her arm and jiggles a new stack of multicolored bangles around her wrist.

"Sweet!" I act happy. *Why shouldn't I be?*

"So what have you bought so far?" She leans in with a smile.

"Nothing."

She shoots me a look of horror.

"Yet," I quickly add. This seems to calm her.

"We have to plan a shopping excursion, ASAP!" She reaches for her menu and points to an entrée for the waiter hovering behind her.

"Sure. Yeah, whenever you want," I agree as I point to lasagna on the menu.

"Ser—ra," Macey whines. "You should be excited. And you don't sound like you're excited. Can you please be *excited?*" Her words trail into a high pitch, her eyes pop wide, and her dark curls bounce.

"I'm excited!" I throw my hands in the air to please her.

She gives me another disapproving look. "I'll get into it, eventually," I promise. "It just seems so—"

"What?" Sam asks, joining our conversation.

"It seems—superfluous." I sip my water.

"That's a big word for you, Sera," Sam says. "Have you been hitting the S.A.T. books?" she asks with a laugh.

I kick her leg underneath the table.

"Will you ever grow up?" she yells.

"You love me," I insist with a smirk.

She rolls her eyes as she always does when she disapproves, but instead of agitating the conversation further, her gaze falls behind me.

I turn. Bishop strolls into the dining room with a shopping bag under his arm.

"You've been shopping, too?" I ask him when he sits on the bench next to me, his back facing the table.

"No, not really." He smiles, handing over the bag.

"What is it, then?" I ask, peeking in.

"A present." His beautiful eyes sparkle, smiling back. "Open it."

I pull out a box. Marbled sage and maroon swirls stretch across the wrapping paper. An emerald-green velvet ribbon encircles the width with a large loopy bow.

"This is so beautiful, I don't even want to open it." I gaze at him, overwhelmed with his thoughtfulness.

"Go ahead." He nudges me playfully.

My hand skims under the tape at the ends. The wrapping paper pops open. Carefully, I set the package on the dining table, reach into the open end, and slide out a hardbound book.

The green crushed velvet cover seems to move with the light. My fingers sweep over the front. The fabric changes hues, from light to dark, with each pass of my hand. I flip the book open. The edges of each page are rough and unfinished, and the paper is thick and textured as though it's handmade.

On the first page, in large hand-printed calligraphy, says the words, "My Seraphina."

"You made this?" I ask in disbelief.

"Keep flipping," he urges.

I slide my hand to the edge, folding my fingertips around the deckle-edged page and flip to a letter—the first love letter he ever wrote to me, the day after our first date, just one of his many beautiful, romantic letters. I carefully flip again and again. The entire book is filled with the love letters he's written. I stop on the last one—the one stolen from me in London.

"How?" I ask, confused.

"I wrote duplicates of each one, knowing that I could give this to you for our first anniversary, but I can't wait that long. So whatever today is will have to do." His hand reaches for mine. "Do you like it?"

"I absolutely adore it," I say, but I don't smile. The gift touches me deeply. I lean into his chest and slide my arms in and under his open blazer, locking my fingers tightly behind his back. The entire room disappears and in my mind, we're alone. I'm huddled into Bishop's strong arms and wrapped in our perfect relationship.

No

19

SELFISH

GUILT SURGES THROUGH ME. AFTER BISHOP gave me the most thoughtful gift I've ever received, I lied to him. I told him that I had plans with Aunt Mona, only so I could face off with Hologram Turner again.

Staring into the classroom mirror, I search for the answer to why I'm so selfish. What's wrong with me? My life is perfect in every way: perfect boyfriend, perfect school, perfect everything. Why do I need to have a mom too? I've gone sixteen years without her. Why can't I just let Terease and the Society of Wanderers hunt Cece and the Underground by themselves? If capable, my mom will come and find me when she's saved.

I *think* she will.

And that's my problem, right there. If she's capable, maybe she won't come to find me. Maybe she doesn't need me the way I need her. If she really has been alive all this time, why hasn't she come looking for me? Given the opportunity, she may never look for me, and I'd lose her in time forever. Because maybe—she *doesn't* care.

The only way I'll know for sure is to find her myself. If I can see her, face-to-face, I can ask her the things I've wondered about since I discovered she was still alive. Then, if she wants to, she can leave.

But at least then I'll know the truth. I need to do this for myself, to know my own truths. I need to be a better fighter, I need the rosary necklace, and I need to find her again.

I stretch out as the hologram machine counts down. "Five. Four. Three. Two. One. Hologram number—thirty-seven—on." The robotic voice announces. A fizzled haze of electricity appears, but something's different. When Hologram Turner solidifies and turns, he's dressed in a pair of slacks, a vest, and a long-sleeve shirt. Not an outfit for fighting.

"What's going on?" I ask, fisting my hands on my hips. "You've changed the hologram."

"I didn't say you'd be fighting the same routine *every* time." He struts forward. "I've seen how you've mastered the other holograms over time. I can't allow you the upper hand, can I?" His eyebrows arch and his lips curl at one side.

"I'm curious," he continues, "what will you do to get this

lovely little relic back?" He reaches into his vest and pulls out the rosary, inspecting it carefully.

"You're changing the agreement!" I yell. It's useful that Bishop will not feel my anger toward a hologram, since the training image isn't a threat.

"There was never an agreement—just me offering you a chance. And I'll change the conditions of that chance if I please." He paces, flexing his muscles. He brushes the cross to his lips.

I just stand and gawk, allowing his actions to play in my head. I quickly realize he never intended to give me back the necklace. After our first match, he realized I might beat him and now, he's switching everything around.

"You win!" I scream the safe words. Hologram Turner smiles before he dematerializes into sparkling dust, and the machine turns off.

Angry, I run out the door of the gymnasium and down the hall into Olde Town. I bolt up the hidden emergency steps to the fourth floor of the Academy. Then I storm down the hall to Turner's apartment.

I don't bother knocking. Instead, I kick the door open and then slam it shut. My fists clench into tight balls when I see Turner. He sits, arms hung lazily over the sides of a leather chair, facing the door.

"Seraphina," he says, knowing the name will fire me up further. "I'd calm down if I were you. That is, if you don't want Bishop to know you're here."

I freeze when he mentions Bishop. He's right. I need to clear my head so I can speak in a mild manner and not alarm my team members. As time wears on, they've become more in tune to my emotions, especially anger and fear.

I close my eyes and inhale deeply, telling myself to relax my shoulders, my jaw, my chest, my arms, and everything down to my toes, just as Mr. Tash taught. In an almost meditative state, I inhale deeply again and open my eyes.

Free of my anger, I take time to survey the room. Dull lights flicker an orange glow on the wall. Stacks of drawings and strange little mechanical inventions sit on nearby tables. Music swirls around the space, Italian opera. The room smells like Turner, a delicious spicy musk.

"I've been expecting you," he says. "Take a seat." He gestures.

I do as he asks, trying not to think about why I've come. The thought will only work me into a frenzy again. I throw myself onto the worn leather couch.

"Gabe lets you keep a beat-up couch?" I ask to distract myself. Any time Gabe notices as much as a scrape on a table in our apartment, he fixes the item and returns it the very next day.

"I don't let him in here. I prefer to choose my own possessions and not be controlled by the Academy," he says, glancing around the mismatched apartment.

"I didn't know we had a choice."

"You always have a choice, Seraphina."

I glance around the large apartment, sensing an empty loneliness throughout.

"Turner—why—why don't you have a team?" I ask in the most tactful voice I can muster.

He stretches his neck, rolling it around on his shoulders, allowing himself time to search for the correct words to explain. "I had a team once," he says, looking sad.

"What happened?"

"I suppose you could say it just didn't work out."

"I'm sorry," I say, because I can see the pain in his eyes.

"How are you able to stay, then?"

He leans forward. "I still have an interest in this life, and I enjoy working as the professor's assistant. And maybe I have a vested hope that my team members will change their minds, however impossible that hope is." He regards me. "Nevertheless, it's nothing for you to worry about, Seraphina, it's not of your doing."

"Please don't call me that. You know it irritates me." I sigh.

"Very well." He stands and sits on the couch next to me, draping his arm behind my back, resting it on a pillow.

I slide away slightly. "Can you please just tell me what you want, so I can leave?"

"What I want," he pauses and leans in, "is for you to stay," he says sheepishly.

"And why on earth would I do that?" I cross my arms. "I can see you have no intention of giving back the rosary."

"I will. I told you I would, but only after you've stayed."

"You've been playing a game, Turner. And it's really starting to bother me. It feels like you're using the necklace as a reason to spend time with me." I hadn't even known the words were true, until I said them out loud. I look over at him with shock.

"Yes," he says softly and looks away. "Of course, you see right through me."

"Turner, you need to stop. Really, I mean it. I'm in love with Bishop. I'm *with* Bishop." I have no intention of hurting his feelings. I do care for Turner, even as much as he annoys me. I start to reach for his hand, to comfort him, but I stop and pull away. It will only give him the wrong idea.

"Just give me a chance, please, you'll see," he pleads softly. His beautiful ashen-gray eyes hold me, locked in a tethered gaze.

"I—I'm sorry." I can't help the guilt I feel with the apology.

He grabs both of my hands, sending goose bumps racing up my arms, the same energy that surged through my body the last time we touched. Turner looks down, noticing the pricks on my skin. My face flushes warm and red, igniting an unusual feeling in my stomach. *This shouldn't be happening. He shouldn't make me feel like this.*

"Seraphina." He whispers my name so gently, the breath from his mouth stirs a stray hair that's loosened from my braid. It tickles my face. He brushes his fingertips to my cheek and just for this moment, I allow myself to look at him, to really see every part of his beautiful face—his slate-colored eyes, angular black brows, the coal-black wavy hair framing his chiseled features.

As if I have no control, my eyes shut, and I inhale his intoxicating spicy musk. In my heart, I see beyond his features and into his beautiful soul: charming and provocative, hidden behind a facade of misplaced anger and hurt. Anger that he desperately wants me to understand but is forbidden to explain. To touch him would release his secrets. To kiss him would set him free. My eyes flutter open. His lips, so full, so enticing, are inches away from mine. They whisper, seducing, drawing me closer.

"I'll show you everything, be everything for you." He gently gathers me into his arms.

My breath hitches in my throat.

"No!" I jump up, looking at him in confusion. Without thinking, I turn to quickly leave.

"Sera, wait!" Turner reaches for me.

I swing open the apartment door.

Perpetua stands on the other side, hand lifted, preparing to knock. She's shocked, taking me in, but she instantly glances into the room. I can only imagine what it must look like with the romantic music and low lighting, and Turner looking as though he was about to kiss me.

"Oh—I'm sorry. I can see I'm interrupting something here." She laughs her evil laugh and relaxes. She peeks into the room again, allowing her eyes to soak up every incriminating detail.

"Don't worry, you aren't." I push past her and stomp down the hall.

"Sera!" Turner shoves around her, chasing me.

So I run.

"Sera," Perpetua yells. "Give my regards to Bishop."

And that's when I hear Turner scream. I turn. Terease swoops in from out of nowhere and grabs his collar, yanking him away.

"What do you think you're doing?" Terease asks him.

He fights without saying a word. Finally, he drops to his knees with his head cradled in his hands, sobbing.

Terease's terrifying eyes find mine. I look on in horror, expecting her to torture my mind with her special brand of fire, but the brain-burning flames never come. I bolt, running.

I'm angry—angry with myself for being so incredibly stupid. What was I even thinking? How could I let myself get lost with him? I don't understand why Terease came for him, but what I do understand is that Turner's a danger to my relationship with Bishop and now, so is Perpetua.

Within a few hours, my guilty conscience has grown. Not only am I lying to Bishop, but I also almost kissed another boy…his brother! I sit on a bench on the second floor in the main atrium staring at my mural, the Seraphina Angel by Leonardo da Vinci. Bishop adores the painting because the time-traveling angel looks like me. But angels don't do the things I do. I sit, wallowing in self-loathing for hours.

Our apartment door creaks open. I hear its unique squeak

from down the hall. I tilt my body to one side and see Sam tiptoeing down the corridor. In her light pink pajamas, she pauses and gracefully sits next to me.

"I know why you're out here."

I continue to stare at the painting without responding. If I talk about what happened tonight, I'm certain I'll cry.

"It would be helpful if you just stayed away from Turner."

"How do you know what's going on?" Several guilty tears escape, plinking into dark spots on my pants leg.

"I see things. I pay attention."

"I promise, I don't want him. I want Bishop." My voice trails into a croak and my eyes well up again.

"What am I going to do?"

№

20

LONDON
EXHIBITION

S AM TILTS HER HEAD, STUDYING MY FACE.
Then she does something she rarely does. She shows com-
passion, leaning in to give me a comforting hug. "If you keep
your distance from Turner, things will get better. I promise."

I believe her; I need to. For an entire night, I allow myself hope that her words are true. I will, from now on, avoid
Turner like the plague, even if he has the rosary. I need to
hold on to what I have, not the glorified dream of my mom. I
find the courage to go back to my apartment with Sam at my
side. Thankfully, Bishop slept through our exchange.

I spend most of the night awake, reading through his love

letters, the ones bound into the emerald velvet book. His words only solidified what I already know to be true—Bishop's amazing.

The next morning, Bishop greets me at my bedroom door as he always does. Encircling me with his long arms, he kisses me sweetly on the cheek. But I can't bear to look into his beautiful green eyes. All I'll see in their reflection is the disappointment I feel for myself. I have to tell him about Turner before Perpetua finds him and regales him with her version of the story.

"You look exhausted." He pulls me closer and squeezes.

"I didn't sleep well," I admit and place my head on his chest.

"I'm sorry to hear that." He strokes my hair, giving me more love than I deserve.

"Are you excited about our wandering trip today?"

"Yes," I say automatically. In truth, I'd pushed it to the back of my mind. We've been listening to night classes on the contrapulator, the machine that allows us to learn while we're sleeping. Last night's classes not only covered the regular school curriculum, such as trigonometry and chemistry, but we also learned the etiquette of the mid-1800s and the history of the London Exhibition in 1862 for the field trip we're taking today.

The London Exhibition was a huge event where inventors, entrepreneurs, and artists of the day exhibited their work. Some 28,000 exhibitors attended from around the world, hoping to promote trade and technology.

There's a knock at the door. Sam glides forward to answer it. A smiling Gabe appears in the doorway with two large white garment bags.

"Good morning, my lovelies!" He bounces into the room. "I have your costumes for today." He hangs them on the top of a door and unzips them. He pulls out a charcoal-gray suit for Bishop and a lavender Victorian dress for me.

"We meet in Olde Town at noon. And—oh—unsweet goodness, Sera, we can't have you meeting 1862 with those awful designer bags under your eyes!" Gabe rushes toward me in a panic.

"How can you notice bags under my eyes that quickly," I ask, touching my face. "You've been here for twenty seconds!"

"It's my job, cupcake!" He approaches, pulls Bishop and me away from each other, and pushes me into my room. He drags me into the bathroom and frantically applies night cream under my eyes.

"Did you even sleep last night?" he asks, smearing green goo over my skin.

"Not much." I cross my arms, annoyed. Really, I want to bat him away, but that would be like hitting a kitten.

"It shows! Well, this will have to do," he says with frustration, giving my face a final look. "As soon as you get back from your field trip, take a nap!" Gabe gives me a hug. "I've gotta run and deliver more costumes."

"Ciao, bella!" He blows a kiss at Sam on his way out the door.

"Are you feeling better this morning?" she asks.

"No, not really, but at least my eyes will look fabulous," I joke and swing my hand through the air, mimicking Gabe.

"Just try to enjoy the day with Bishop." For some reason, she's become very sensitive to my feelings. Even though I can't explain it, it's nice to have someone to talk to. If only I could talk to her about everything else.

"I'll try."

She leaves, and I hop in the shower. Afterward, I dry my hair and twist it into a pile of curls on top of my head. To complete the style, I pin a delicate charcoal-colored hat adorned with mounds of lavender ribbon on top. The hairstyle matches exactly with a photo given to me by Gabe—his idea of a quickie beauty manual for the 1860s.

I step into a crinoline and pull it to my waist; the multiple layers sway with each step and will give the lower half of my dress its bell shape. Sam arrives to help tie off the corset. It's awful and binding, but part of the costume. Finally, she helps me into the silk dress. With all the fabric, the thing weighs a ton, and the added weight of the crinoline doesn't help. Sam fastens the opal buttons on the front. There are at least fifty of them, starting at my stomach and ending just below a lacy ruffled collar around my neck.

"Does it make you sad that you never get to dress up?" I ask. As our Seer, she remains in this time period, true time.

As Bishop and I wander back into history, she'll fall into a meditative state, in which she'll view our travels through Bishop's mind. They're connected like a chain—her to him and he to me.

"A little. Even though I can't travel with you physically, in my mind I feel as though I'm experiencing everything. It's the most vivid dream you can imagine." She finishes buttoning the top button.

She turns and reaches for a set of earrings, a pretty teardrop pair that dangle. When I put them on, they brush my jawline.

"You look perfect!"

"Thanks. Um—are you okay? I mean—you've been acting different. Sort of." Nicer really, although, I don't want to say that to her face.

"Fine." She forces a flat smile. Obviously, she's not.

"Seraphina, it's time to go." Bishop enters my room. He's dashing and regal in his charcoal-gray gentleman's suit, cut in a Victorian style. And just now, I notice that he's grown sideburns. The look suits him.

"You're lovely." He presents his arm.

"Oh, almost forgot." Sam reaches for something on the dresser. "Here's your relic for the day." She hands it to Bishop. "It's an original ticket to the London Exhibition, the day it opened." The ticket is black leather with gold letters embossed on the face. The logo of the exhibition building stretches across the top.

"Should be a fairly simple ride, not too many bumps in the wormhole," she explains.

Sam's grown intimately attuned to her job as Seer, learning about relics and finding the quickest route to any event in time. She turns to leave, heading for the Seer's meditation room.

·

Students line up around the edge of Olde Town. Ms. Midgenet stands at the front of the line, offering final bits of advice as teams prepare to wander back in time.

When it's our turn, we step forward.

"Okay, let's see what we have here." Miss Midgenet inspects us. "Gabe's meeting you on the other side. Here's some time-appropriate money and a guide booklet, listing the exhibitors." She hands me a small change purse and the booklet. I tuck them into my drawstring purse. "I see you have your relic." She nods at the ticket in Bishop's hand. "And your keyword is 'the London Exhibition of 1862.' All right?"

We nod.

"Any other questions?"

"No," we say.

"Well then, off you go!" She waves. A long patio of stone, perfect for running, stretches before us. Bishop holds the relic ticket in his hand and the keyword in his mind. Combined, they'll transport us to the moment the relic and keyword crossed paths in history. Bishop gives me a gentle tug, and we run across the courtyard hand in hand.

The usual happens. Behind us, Olde Town folds up like a wave. The floor that we once ran over hovers above for several moments before crashing down, smacking us into a time-traveling wormhole.

The ride doesn't make me sick like it used to. In fact, I find a strange peace in the transition. A blinding light appears at the far end of the tunnel. Like a magnet, we're pulled forward and spit out. We land on a patch of dirt, where several students gather.

"Come, come, move out of the way before the next team pops through." Gabe beckons.

"Sera, over here!" Macey waves in our direction.

As we approach, I notice something different. Macey and Xavier are holding hands. I flash her a grin, happy that she's finally chosen one of the boys and put the other out of his lovesick misery.

She rolls her eyes, knowing full well what I've zeroed in on. "Come on, Xavier." She pulls him away before I can say anything. She turns and whispers, "We'll chat later."

"I hope so!" I call after her.

"What was that about?" Bishop asks.

"She's finally picked one."

"One, what?"

"Ya know, one of her team members. They're both in love with her. She finally chose one."

"Attention, everyone!" Gabe interrupts our conversation as he engages the crowd of students. "Now that you're all here, please remember a few things. It's 1862, not true time, my lovelies. Mingle and have fun exploring all that the exhibition has to offer, but please observe from afar with minimal interaction. Consider each exhibit and how it's changed our society. The inventions, the technology, the arts here have shaped the world you and I know. It's a very exciting time," Gabe says with exuberance.

"We meet back here in three hours. Please set your timepieces." Each team complies.

"And most of all, have a fabulous time!" he says, clasping his hands.

A few teams at a time, we walk toward the Exhibition Hall. Many people linger in the building's vicinity. There's a feeling of busyness, which I can only compare to the excitement of Times Square in New York. Instead of yellow taxis and honking horns, horse's hooves clip-clop, kicking up clouds of dust. Ornate buggies clatter and clank behind them.

Bishop and I stand in the entrance line. Looking around, I admire the grand exhibition building. Large arched windows wrap the facade. An oversized dome soars above the roofline, reaching for the sky. Several flags, mounted on poles, whip and crack in the breeze.

The line moves briskly toward a grand arched entrance where an attendant waves us in when Bishop flashes our gilded ticket. Upon entry, the stifling air surrounds us. So many people cram into the space that it's uncomfortable. I pull at my high lace collar, loosening the fabric.

Bishop tugs my arm, guiding me into smaller exhibit area. Thankfully, there are less people, and it's cooler here with the windows propped open. The corridor arches several stories high. A banner hangs from the ceiling, emblazoned MACHIN-ERY IN MOTION.

We've entered an industrial exhibit area. About fifty stands have nothing but sewing machines. Each machine has its own special design, but it's easy to pick out the designs that work best. These are the ones that resemble the sewing machines we have in true time.

As we stroll, the machines become larger. Steam engines blow smoke into the air, printing presses show the speed at which a book can be printed, the Platt Brothers demonstrate textile manufacturing. We're amazed to see plastic, or at least the first manmade version of it, at its debut.

"There's a similar exhibit in the Science Museum in London, in true time," Bishop tells me.

"It's actually more interesting to observe the people. Their faces say it all," I say and point to a group of men huddled around a steam engine. "Look at their expressions." I giggle. "They're in awe of these machines, as if they're magic."

"'Any sufficiently advanced technology is indistinguishable from magic,'" Bishop recites. At my confused look, he adds, "Arthur C. Clarke."

"That quote makes me think of science fiction, space ships, robots, and stuff. But I guess that speaks to any time in history, not just ours."

"Indeed, it does." Bishop wraps my hand around his arm.

We step into a new section. There's art, sculpture, literature, music, and fashion from every imaginable place on earth. Beautiful urns and jars stack high. Exquisite jewelry glitters behind glass display cases, cases so beautiful and ornate, their woodworked craftsmanship should be appreciated as well.

We explore for a couple of hours, admiring everything. But after so much walking, I'm tired and sore from carrying the weight of the dress. We sit on the edge of an enormous, intricately carved fountain.

Bishop flips through the guidebook and sighs. "Clearly, we'll never see everything," he says as he snaps it shut.

"No, but maybe we can come back another time, just the two of us." As I say the words, I see Perpetua some distance away, strolling with Stu. She turns in our direction and smirks when she sees us. No doubt, she's remembering the dirt she thinks she has on Turner and me. With a calculating expression, she promptly turns and heads our way.

No 21

UNFRAG-MENTATION

I PANIC BECAUSE I HAVE YET TO DECIDE HOW TO approach the problematic subject with Bishop. First, I'd have to explain why I was in Turner's room last night. Second, that would lead to a lot of other questions that I'm not prepared to answer.

Before Bishop can spot Perpetua, I jump up and drag him away into a grouping of palm trees that encircles a large obelisk. "Do you think it means we have relatives here?" I point at the monument, feigning interest.

"There's a high likelihood of other Wanderers, I'm sure."

I glance over my shoulder; Perpetua moves closer.

"Let's investigate!" I drag him past the obelisk in a very unladylike way that makes people gasp and point. We duck behind a wall of red-fringed curtains. Before we get too far, a large man who reminds me of a bouncer grabs each of us by the arm.

"Where do you think you're going?" he asks in a rough voice, casting a disapproving look from under the rim of his hat. "This part of the exhibit's private."

"They're fine." A young boy places his hand on the man's arm, easing him away.

The man inspects us and finally nods. "Go on."

Bishop and I eye the boy. He's thirteen at best and certainly not someone who would normally give orders.

The boy appraises the look on our faces. "You're like me," he says.

"What do you mean, like you?" I cross my arms.

He shrugs with an enigmatic expression and waves for us to follow.

We pass through a second set of curtains. On the other side, many people crowd in front of a large stage. In the spotlight, a man in his thirties stands next to an enormous contraption, identifying the details for the audience.

"A relicutionist!" I point. The machine is similar to the Academy's, but larger, perhaps an older model.

"See, you are one of us." The boy turns and smiles.

"Yes, but how did you know?" Bishop asks.

"It's my gift," the boy answers. He might be a hybrid like

Terease, a Wanderer with special abilities.

I smile at the boy. "You're American?"

"Yes. I'm here from Chicago, with my father." He gestures to the man on the stage. "He's an inventor. I want to be like him one day." He turns. "My name is Elijah."

"I'm Bishop and this is Sera." Bishop gestures to me, making the introduction.

"Nice to meet you." He smiles and shakes each of our hands like an adult, then glances over his shoulder to his dad. The man waves him forward. "Wait here," he says, then trails away and hops onto the stage.

"It's Vanderpool. Sam's just confirmed it," Bishop leans over and whispers.

"The boy?" I gasp. Elijah Vanderpool is the founding father of our school, an important figure in our Wandering history.

"Sam just told me that Eli's father's name is Macon," Bishop continues. "He invented the early versions of the relicutionist and contrapulator, among many other important Wandering inventions. After Elijah grew up and built Olde Town, he carried on his father's work. That must be his mom, Hannah Louise, there." He points to a woman partially hidden behind the curtains.

Two men roll the relicutionist off stage. A massive new machine the size of a small truck is wheeled on, a huge glass box that sits on wagon wheels. Cranks, pipes, and levers from an engine protrude from three sides.

"And this," Macon says, addressing the crowd and waving

his hand at the machine, "is the unfragmentation machine. It takes fragmented relics and returns them to their original state!" The crowd, obviously filled with Wanderers, presses forward, chattering with excitement.

Fragmented relics are those relics that have been broken. They're unusable to Wanderers because their time-traveling life paths are scrambled and can send you anywhere in time. In other words, they're useless.

"Allow me to demonstrate!" Macon says. His wife, Hannah, steps onstage, handing him an ornate vase. He gently places the vase on a stand for everyone to see. Little Elijah appears with a hammer and presents it to his father. With the hammer in hand, Macon takes one quick whack at the vase. Several broken sections crack and crumble into an unrecognizable mess.

Hannah steps forward again and gathers the shards into a square of cloth. She carefully places the shards in the glass box of the unfragmentation machine. She shuts the door tightly, locking it shut.

All together, the trio's timing is perfect, and I can't help thinking that I'm watching a skilled magician perform with his assistants.

Macon rotates the large lever on the side of the contraption. At first, there's only a slow, repetitious cranking noise. The gears grind and rotate, building momentum. A whistle screams like a train. The crowd jolts. The floor shakes, tickling the soles of my feet within my boots. I grasp Bishop's arm, hoping, praying that the machine doesn't blow. These are early Wandering experiments, after all. There's no telling how safe they truly are.

Gray smoke fills the glass box. The smoke creeps and drifts in long, undulating fingers until it meets the vase. Then, like a snake, it coils around the object, engulfing its mass in a rotating cloud of blue electrical sparks. Static electricity zaps and pops, stimulating the pieces, causing them to vibrate. The shards rise, airborne, caught in the circular wind of a miniature tornado. Violently, they spin until they've reconstructed themselves into one piece. As good as new, the vase hovers in the glass box.

The crowd breaks into applause.

"Ah! But that's not all!" Macon assures everyone in a very carny manner. "Suppose you don't have all the pieces to a broken relic? Hmm? What do you do then?" He looks around the crowd, pretending to search for someone who might have the answer.

There's a low murmur in response.

"Well, don't fret, I'll show you what can be done." Macon starts the demonstration over with the same vase. This time, after smashing it, instead of putting *all* the pieces into the glass case, he hands one large shard to Elijah.

"Sera, come forward." Elijah beckons me to the stage.

The crowd parts, clearing a path to the stage. Bishop and I move forward.

"Hold out your hands," Elijah instructs. I do as he asks,

and he places the shard in my cupped, gloved hands. "Just hold it right here, up high, so everyone can see," he explains and steps away.

With the audience satisfied that I hold a real piece of the broken vase, Macon starts the machine again. The unfragmentation machine functions exactly the same as before, but this time, when the tornado spins within the case, melding the pieces back together, the shard in my hand disappears into thin air. It reappears in the case, miraculously returning the vase to its original glory.

I gasp and lift my now empty hands in disbelief. The unfragmentation machine can pull pieces from anywhere to reconstruct a fragmented relic. I immediately understand that this machine is extremely powerful. I wonder if the machine still exists in true time. And if so, where it is.

The crowd of Wanderers breaks into a large roar of applause; shrill whistles of appreciation pierce the air.

"Pretty amazing, right?" Perpetua whispers in my ear.

I stiffen, realizing she's followed us and made it past the bouncer.

No 22

PERPETUA

AFTER THE DEMONSTRATION, BISHOP DROPS my hand and drifts to Elijah to chat. He hasn't noticed Perpetua in the commotion and excitement of the crowd.

"Yeah, it's awesome," I respond to Perpetua in a monotone.

"You know what else is awesome, Sera?"

"No." I grit my teeth.

"Watching you squirm every time I come around you now. You just never know when I'll spill what I know about you and Turner to your lover boy, do you?" She laughs.

Ticked beyond comprehension, I spin to face her. I lift

my fists to rip her face off but she's gone, disappeared in the crowd. I weave around the bodies, looking for her. At the back of the room, I find a wooden box and stand on it. Now elevated, I spot her. She's at the front of the room, standing next to Bishop and leaning to whisper into his ear.

My heart stops. *She lured me away*. Without a thought, I run for them, bulldozing through the crowd, hoping to defend myself from whatever crap she's spouted. Whatever she's said, it won't be easy to explain away.

When I arrive, Stu, her Wanderer, has joined them. I crash into them like a renegade bowling ball, knocking down pins.

"Sera, are you all right?" Bishop catches me before I hit the floor.

"I can explain, I promise." Desperately, I plant a kiss on his lips, wrap my arms around his shoulders, and hang on for dear life.

"Explain what?" He stares down into my eyes, confused.

I shoot Perpetua a look of shock. She smirks. "We were just discussing this amazing machine." She gestures to the stage. "Do you know how it works, Sera?" She cocks her head. She hasn't told Bishop anything, not yet. She's enjoying messing with me too much.

Ninety-nine percent of me wants to rage at her, but one percent, a small voice of sanity, holds me back. "Let's go, Bishop." I grab his hand and pull him away. If I keep looking at her face, I won't be able to control myself.

"Sera, wait! What's wrong? Is she still pestering you about her crystal? If so, I'll make her stop, don't worry." Bishop turns to confront her.

"No, that's not it." I press my palms into his chest, holding him back.

"Is everything okay? You're acting strange." He stops to survey me.

"Stranger than normal?" I ask, subduing my true feelings. Every time I look at him, I realize just how much I suck. He's too good for me in so many ways.

"No, I suppose not." He relaxes and smiles, then leans down to kiss me. We receive a few gasps at our public display of affection. When we realize our faux pas, we pull apart and quickly fall back into character, returning to our refined and subdued nineteenth-century alter egos.

For the small amount of time we have left at the exhibition, I do my best to stay out of Perpetua's way. It's not like me to run away from bullies, but I really need to decide how to deal with her. I need time to think.

•

My thoughts run wild well into the next day. In fact, I've spent the last twenty hours analyzing everything that's wrong with myself. Even with my endless internal dialog, I've yet to determine the perfect solution.

Somehow, I have to figure out how to tell Bishop about my mounting secrets. First, I need to talk to him about Turner, before Perpetua does. That discussion will lead to my next secret——that I've become a better fighter, which I need to reveal before Ms. Swift's class on Friday. And last, but not least, he needs to know that I've been looking for my mom.

In my heart, I know I've hidden the truth only because I've wanted to protect him from being hurt on so many levels. His body from being physically hurt by the Underground again, his ego from my wanting to become a better fighter, and his heart from my friendship with Turner. I've had my reasons, yes…but are they admirable ones? Something within my soul fights fiercely to protect Bishop at any cost, and I don't understand why.

For today's class, Relics II, I hope I can get lost in my studies and avoid everyone until I can answer that question.

Argus Matchimus, the curator, stands before us in the enormous archive of relics. Somehow, I always expect the room to look smaller, but it never does. Rows and rows of wooden shelving, whose end I can't see, hold ancient artifacts. Each contains endless amounts of histories within their life paths.

Argus waddles amongst the students, his voice as rough as sandpaper, and welcomes us back for our second year. After a short speech, he sends us on our way with instructions to explore the archives on our own. He escapes to a nearby desk in a dark corner and proceeds to eat a pastry.

Perpetua strategically sits nearby, taunting me with her evil gaze. She pops up and sashays over to my team, dropping a palm on Bishop's shoulder.

"Bishop, we must chat soon and catch up!" she says with bubbly exuberance. He tenses under her touch, and her eyes dart to me. "And how are you doing today, Sera? Sleep well?" Her lips tug at one corner.

"Slept great." I smile, disguising my distress.

"I bet you did," she says, pushing our game further. How long will she torture me? She struts off with Stu and Jessica.

"Perpetua's getting annoying. Why can't she just leave you alone?" Sam asks, typing on the computer.

"*Getting* annoying? Hasn't she always been?" I ask.

"Yeah, she's a mega-witch." Macey walks over, joining the conversation.

I snort with laughter. "Something like that."

"So when can we go shopping, Sera? I need to get out of this hole and have some fun. You're so serious these days," Macey complains and sits.

"Just name the time and place, chick."

"This Saturday, before the dance. Let's go get our hair done."

"My hair is looking pretty drab these days," I admit.

Bishop picks up a strand of my hair. "You should add that strip of color back in," he suggests.

"Maybe," I consider. If I weren't mentally fighting my self-serving ways, I might relax a little and just be a teenager for once. The conversation dies, and I type random letters into the computer, pretending to be engaged in classroom studies.

Seers sit on the floor in meditative states. Relics float

above their cupped palms, bathing in warm glows, revealing their life paths. Wanderers and Protectors stand in line to use the relicutionist, the machine that reads relics and visually shows their life paths like a movie.

Needing more of a distraction, I stroll to no place in particular through the archives and find myself at row eighty-nine. I turn right and stop at a box at eye level. When I remove the wooden case, Perpetua stands on the other side, peeking through the shelf. She followed me.

"I guess it's better if we chat back here," she says and leans in, resting her arms on the shelf and dropping her chin into her hand. She blows one long breath and a whirl of dust billows into the air.

I cough. "What do you want?" I sit the box on the floor and stand to face her. I school my face into a hard expression to hide my guilt.

"Well, I thought long and hard about this, but I wanted to discuss it with you first," she says as though she's going to present an offer.

"And what's that, exactly?"

"It would be so easy to run tell Bishop what I saw between you and Turner, but where would be the fun in that?" she considers with a malicious chuckle.

"I don't know what you think you saw but nothing happened."

"I know what I saw, and when I investigated further, Bishop informed me that you spent that evening with your aunt.

So I think he'd be surprised to learn the truth. Don't you?"

"What do you want?" My cool facade's crumbling fast.

"You know what I want."

"I already told you, I don't know anything about your stupid rock."

"I understand," she says with fake sympathy, "but you will. And more importantly, you'll find it, or I'll tell Bishop the truth." Her voice sings with evil excitement.

"I don't even know what the thing looks like."

"We'll chat later." She walks away, waving over her shoulder and disappears.

Bishop appears next to me and crouches down to open the box I pulled from the shelves.

"What was that about?" he asks, as he pops the latch and raises the lid.

"Nothing, you know how she is. Blah, blah, blah, where's my crystal?" I say, hoping to appear unfazed.

"Right. Are you sure you don't want me to say anything?"

I crouch next to him. "Positive. There's nothing I can do any—"

A forceful explosion rips through the air, tossing Bishop and me across the room. We crash into a shelf of relics and fall into a heap on the dusty floor.

S HELVES COLLAPSE OVER US. CLAY POTS, GLASS miniatures, and thousand-year-old relics smash, shattering on the floor. Bishop wraps his arms around my body and drags me away from the debris. Thick green smoke with the smell of rotting garbage makes visibility difficult. Students scream in the distance. Shocked and confused, I don't understand what's happening.

I lift myself, pulling away from Bishop, but there's nowhere to go. We're stuck underneath a wooden teepee made of archive shelving.

"We need to get out of here!" I'm forced to yell because

of the din that surrounds us. People are screaming, some in pain. Others add to the cacophony with grunts, thuds, and crashes. The sounds of combat.

"You're hurt," Bishop says. I look down. Blood soaks through my sleeve. Now that I see it, pain shoots through my arm. Bishop props me against the wall, rips off a piece of his shirt, and wraps it around my wound, tying the fabric in a tight knot.

"We need to keep pressure on it." He squeezes.

"It's nothing, really, we need to help!"

The screaming and sounds of fighting continue. We hear shouting, as more people arrive, hopefully the Society Security, the ones sent to protect us. Bishop and I push the bookshelves, attempting to lift them, but they won't budge, not one inch.

"Over there!" I point to a small opening. "I think we can crawl through." I scramble on hands and knees, ignoring the pain.

I crawl through the newly made tunnel of shelves that runs along the outer walls of the Relic Archives. Near the end, I squeeze through a smaller opening, scraping my bad arm on the edge of a shelf, and pull myself into the open air. The putrid smoke has cleared somewhat, allowing more visibility. We're at the back of the archives, far from the fighting.

I race to the combat zone and immediately collide with a foul-smelling man, whom I can only presume is a member of the Underground. He takes a quick whack at me with his club, engaging me in battle. I land a few decent blows before Bishop hurls me out of the way, taking my place.

Atticus flies across the room, landing nearby. A woman covered in tattoos and piercings jumps him and pounds his head. I leap with a running start and launch my feet at her body. Upon impact, she soars through the air.

Like a cat, she lands on her feet. She turns her attention to me, leaving Atticus out of harm's way. She attacks, lodging her shoulder into my stomach, ramming me until my back crashes against the wall. The impact knocks the air out of me. Her hands clench my neck and squeeze. I kick and thrash, doing anything I can to push her away, but my vision begins to blur.

I stab my thumbs into her eyes. She falters, and then I jab a knee into her rib cage. She steps away, screaming in pain, and I slam my elbow into her chest for another blow. This sends her back a few paces, but she's the resilient type. Even though her eyes are bleeding, she charges again.

Punch. Jab. Kick. Spin. My fist shatters her face several times. And then, when I momentarily have the upper hand, I consider her weakness. It's staring me in the face, literally shining. I grab the chain connected from her nose to her earring and rip it from her skin.

She screams in hideous pain, simultaneously grabbing her head and ear. One last swift kick sends her hurling across the room. She plunges back, smashing her head onto the rubble. Her lifeless body dangles over a shelf.

When I spin to see how I can help the next person, I notice Ms. Swift standing in the war zone, machete in hand, smiling. She's seen what I can do and now, I realize, so has Bishop. The adrenaline that's been surging through my veins while fighting turns heavy like a drug. The high crashes into a depressing low. I turn, searching for Bishop, immediately wanting to explain myself.

The foul-smelling man clenches Bishop in a headlock; I hurdle over debris to come to his aid. Angry, I throw my knee into the man's lower back. There's a sickly crack of his spine. The man folds in half backward before he hits the ground. Bishop rolls away and leaps to his feet, safe. I run to him and throw my arms around his shoulders, but the moment is short. He jolts, then pulls himself away and jerks his head from side to side, scanning the rubble.

"Sam!" Bishop screams. He takes off looking for her, searching for her familiar mind.

The smoke has completely cleared, and I can see that the fighting has mostly stopped. Society guards have overwhelmed the surviving Underground stragglers and work to restrain them. Students lie scattered around the floor, some moaning. With so many bodies, I don't even know what to do first.

I panic.

I run to the person lying closest to me. Atticus. I hadn't noticed how bad his injuries were before, but now I see. He's bruised and bloody, barely alive. Scarlett lays nearby, a lump on the ground. She's still breathing, but her arm is mangled and broken. Agnes rushes to their aid, but she can barely contain her tears.

The room becomes crowded as teachers and school medics stream in, ready to help.

In the distance, Bishop lifts Sam upright. I breathe in relief, happy for her safety.

"Sera," a weak, but familiar, voice says. My eyes search for Macey. Her bloody hand reaches for me.

"Mace!" I climb over mounds of debris, making my way to her.

Her lower body is pinned under a large bookcase. I strain to lift it, but it's too heavy.

"Bishop!" I yell. "Help, someone!" Several hands come to my aid, and together we lift the massive shelf. I let them hold the considerable weight momentarily while I crouch down to pull her out from the rubble.

"Does anything hurt?" I lean down to her and stroke her hair to keep her calm as I quickly try to assess her injuries.

"Think I'm okay, but Quinn. His leg is stuck under a rock, over there somewhere." She points.

I jump over her and yell his name.

A cracked voice croaks from behind a pile of debris.

"Quinn?"

I rush to him and lean into a rock that once lined the wall, pushing it off his leg with all my weight. Quinn screams in horrific pain. A Society medic arrives and immediately kneels down to help him. I step out of the way and turn to scan the room for others needing help.

My heart races when I see Turner. He's wounded, sitting propped up in the corner with Sam just arriving to help him. I rush to him and drop to my knees. There's a bloody gash in his shirt, several inches long.

"You weren't even in this class. How did you get hurt?" When I lift his shirt, I see his skin is a gnarled, bloody mess.

He and Sam exchange a look that I can't make sense of. I gently touch the wounded area and Turner screams. "Sam, go find help," I say. She nods and scampers away.

"Well? Why are you here?" I shrug out of my vest, then bundle the fabric, pressing it firmly over his wound to stem the blood loss.

"To protect," he moans.

Bishop appears. "Sera, go have the school nurse look at your arm. I'll take care of Turner." He lifts me up and pushes me aside.

"I'm fine!" I glance down at my arm. It's worse than before. Blood drains from my face, sending cold chills racing down my back. My body temperature drops, causing gray dots to multiply before my eyes. Finally, my world turns to dark silence.

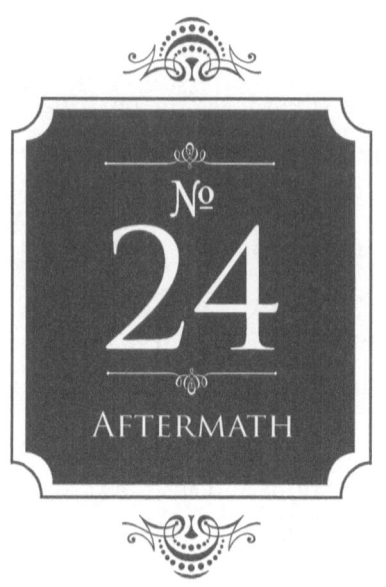

№ 24

AFTERMATH

I WAKE IN A MAKESHIFT HOSPITAL. AT LEAST FIFTY
temporary cots line a hallway of the Academy. I look down.
My arm is clean and bandaged. Sam sits at the end of the cot,
rolling her long braid between her fingers.

"How are you feeling?"

"I'm fine." I sit up, still feeling woozy.

"You blacked out, probably from shock."

I swing my legs over the side of the bed, feet skimming the
floor.

"Is everyone all right?" Visions of several injured students,
Macey, Quinn, Atticus, and Turner, flash through my mind.

"They'll be fine," she assures me. "You should lay back down and rest."

I look around, too angry to relax.

Nearby, Terease stands at a hole in the wall the size of a small car. Stones crumble at its edges as though it were blasted through with explosives. The mound of debris behind it used to be someone's apartment.

Because I can't contain my anger, I stand and stomp toward Terease. She's speaking with a Society soldier. "Why did the Underground do this?" I interrupt.

"That's none of your concern," Terease snaps.

"Look around you! My friends are hurt. It concerns all of us! I think it's time you really start explaining what's going on!" I yell.

She narrows her eyes, holding her usual air of superiority, giving herself several seconds before she responds. "Yes, you're right. I suppose it's time to stop sheltering all of you. We'll make arrangements for an assembly as soon as we're organized and secure."

Shocked at Terease's willingness to agree, I only nod. I had prepared myself mentally for an argument. Disregarding me, she returns to her conversation with the soldier. Sam grabs my shoulders and guides me back to the cot.

"Just rest a little longer," she urges.

I do as she says and rest with my eyes shut, pretending to sleep. When I sense Sam leave, I sit up again and scan the students sleeping on nearby cots. None of them are my close friends, and none are Turner.

I stand and explore the halls, assessing the devastation. Most of it appears internal. The Underground ransacked the school looking for something. With the amount of damage, I realize the fighting must have gone on well before they found their way to the Relic Archives. We just never heard the commotion so deep underground.

Society soldiers guard every exit. They've sent more since the attack. I manage to find a window to peek out. Hundreds of people mill around the courtyard. Most of them appear to be reporters, police officers, or emergency personnel.

Mr. Evanston, the headmaster of the Academy, stands outside giving some kind of media conference—*damage control.* Who knows what lies he's telling the Normals to cover up an attack of this magnitude. How will they keep the Feds from investigating? The Society probably has people on the inside there, too. Wanderer double agents, just to smooth over incidents like this—scary, but probably true.

After a while, I find Bishop sitting on the floor, shoulders slumped, leaning heavily against the wall behind him. He's staring blankly at a painting in the main atrium. I drop to the floor beside him, cuddling into his side, and he pulls me close. Students shuffle past, some covered in stone dust and with minor injuries that have been attended to; others are in better shape, but wear the same dazed expression. Like me, they're probably struggling to find answers to the purpose of this chaos and destruction. Why? Why would the Underground do this? We're just a school, nothing in the grand scheme of things. What were they looking for?

"How are you feeling?" Bishop gently runs his fingers around the edge of my tangled hair.

"Not great," I admit with a sigh.

"Sam told me you were resting."

"Too upset."

"Yeah, me too," he mumbles.

"How's Turner?"

He stiffens slightly at Turner's name. "At the hospital, getting stitched up and pumped full of antibiotics, but he'll be fine. Our father's traveling from London to be with him."

"And everyone else?"

"Quinn, Scarlett, and Atticus are at the Normals' hospital, as well. Their injuries were too severe to treat here. But everyone will be okay. The Society soldiers fought off most of the attack until the Underground snuck into the archives. That's where most of the students were hurt." He pauses thoughtfully. "You fought very well," he says softly and looks away.

"Yeah," I mumble. I hide my eyes in the curve of his neck. I hadn't thought my actions through; I just jumped in to help. He knows now, finally, that I'm a good fighter. After all, he's seen me in action.

"I'm glad," he says and kisses my forehead. He gives me a weary hug and says no more. But I know he's hurt. Not in the way a Normal's pride would be, but only in the way a Protector can be. Still, I always underestimate his selflessness. He just lets his troubled feelings go—for me. Everything he does is for me.

He's too good for me because, even now, I can't bring myself to tell him about my mom, to tell him she's alive, and that I want to go back and kick Cece's butt to save her. With this attack, my resolve is even stronger.

No

25

TWO
HEARTS

FOR THE SECOND NIGHT IN A ROW, I'M THRUST out of a restless sleep. A sheen of chilly sweat encases my body. The hair at the nape of my neck is soaked and coiled around my shoulder and onto my back. The contrapulator, sensing my elevated heart rate, turns off, and I remove the attached headphones from my ears.

Sitting up, I squint at the antique clock—just past three in the morning. I press the heels of my palms into my eyes, trying as I have many times before to rub the thoughts of the attack and every other problem I've created for myself out of my head. But they're lodged there, tormenting me.

Before I can allow the memories to encroach further, I roll

out of bed and change my clothes. Sam and Bishop are asleep in their rooms when I slip out the front door. There's only one place that can alleviate the nightmares. The only place I feel stronger and in control—the defense training room.

·

I pace the room, lunging and swiping a sword through the air while the hologram machine counts down, starting from five. When the electrical current flutters, stimulating a solid mass into being, I'm hoping to fight something mean and nasty to get my mind off things. But I quickly realize that Turner's changed all my training holograms—not just the new ones. I should have expected it. I huff in annoyance and collapse to the floor, frustrated.

Hologram Turner turns and smiles. He strolls forward and sits on the floor in front of me. In real life, he's in the hospital, the gash in his abdomen too serious for him to be released yet.

"I thought you might drop in here again." He smirks.

"Yes, but I didn't know I'd be forced to face *you* every time. Where are my old training holograms?"

"Gone. I needed to make sure I had a chance to apologize." He plays with his cuff, acting more vulnerable than I've ever seen him. Maybe Hologram Turner is better than the real thing.

"So I'm supposed to accept an apology from a hologram?" I snort.

"It's still me." He looks up from under his dark lashes.

"I can't wait to hear this, go ahead." I gesture to him, playing along.

He pauses, considering his words. "How can you blame

me—for wanting to be near you—for wanting to love you? Is that such a crime?" he asks seriously.

I look around, uncomfortable. He's so much freer with his emotions, so eager to get them off his chest. Unlike Bishop, who took months to tell me he loved me, Turner says the words easily but with the same conviction. "That's a strange apology."

"Well, it's the truth. I guess it's not really an apology. How can I apologize for loving you?" he asks, holding my gaze with his.

I sigh heavily and drop my shoulders, finding myself feeling sorry for him. "I'm sorry. It just can't be." Sam's right. I need to stay away from him.

"You realize," he pauses, "it won't change the way I feel. I can't change it."

"Find someone else," I blurt.

"It would only mask the truth."

"So then, what? What do you suggest?"

"I suggest nothing." He smiles, but it doesn't reach his eyes as he says softly, "I'm with you, or I'm nothing."

Just as I reach out to comfort him, he says, more firmly, "You win."

My fingers sizzle with the electricity of the fleeting hologram. His mass shimmers, sparkling in air, and Hologram Turner disappears.

All alone, I scream from sadness and frustration. I'm hurting someone and there's nothing I can do about it. In fact, Turner's letting me hurt him, and I don't even understand why.

I clench my fists until my nails cut into my palms.

"Volta Swift!" I scream.

"Volta Swift," the hologram machine repeats calmly. "Locating routines now." The machine scrolls. "Hologram—number—fifty—requires no weapons—hologram starts in—thirty seconds. Safe words are—'you win.'"

I roll to a standing position, waiting for the next monster to appear—one of Ms. Swift's training routines. I know Turner hasn't messed with hers. I'm ready to rip out another hologram's heart. It seems that's what I do best.

The next morning, I awake to Sam shaking my bed.

"Sera, wake up."

"Ugh. Leave me alone. Why won't you let me sleep?" I tug the covers over my head and roll toward the wall. I hadn't gotten into bed until six in the morning.

"It's your Dad. Um, he's here."

"Here?" I sit up clutching the covers, and stare at her through sleepy eyes.

She nods nervously.

When I stumble out of my bedroom, blanket wrapped around my shoulders, Ray rushes from the front door where he's been pacing and embraces me. "Oh, thank goodness you're okay!" He hugs me tightly to his chest; I can feel his heart beating wildly and the slight tremor in his hand as he awkwardly strokes my hair.

For a moment, I think I'm dreaming. This is obviously some parallel universe. Ray hugging me like this is stranger than Wandering. "Yes. I'm—I'm fine," I stammer in shock and stiffen slightly in his arms, so unaccustomed to being there.

He holds me away from his face, gripping my arms. I wince as he presses the wound beneath my shirt. "I saw the news. What happened? They're saying it was an explosion. Why didn't you call me?" He rushes his words in frantic bursts.

I hadn't prepared myself for this conversation. Never even dreamed it would happen. "Dad!" I pull myself from his grasp and walk away to plop on the couch, preparing to give him the speech we were instructed to tell our Normal parents about the Underground's attack on the school. It never occurred to me that mine would even care. "It was nothing, just a student prank gone wrong. We're perfectly safe."

He assesses me. "You weren't involved were you?" And... now we're back to the Ray I know and love.

"No! Of course not!" I force out a huff of air in a grunt.

"Well, whatever it was, I've decided I'm taking you home. I don't like you being here anymore. Obviously, it's not safe." He looks around, eyeing Bishop and Sam, who are standing in their bedroom doorways wearing their pajamas, their faces impassive and arms crossed.

"Dad, I'm fine. You're totally overreacting."

"No, I'm not. Get your things together. We're leaving today."

This can't be happening. I'm too tired for this. I just stare at him, unable to budge. My annoyance and frustration skyrocket; I can feel my face tighten, unable to hide the emotions.

"Seraphina, I said now!" He points to the floor for emphasis.

"No!" I drop the blanket and jump to my feet, squaring up to face him with my fists clenched with determination.

"I'm not going to say it again. I'm leaving, and you're coming with me."

"There's no way, Dad. I have friends here."

"You'll make new friends."

"I have a family here!" I yell, going right for the jugular. "You couldn't pay me to leave this life. They actually want to be around me—unlike you," I snap, and then step back, shocked that I've actually said the words out loud. They hang in the air for several seconds, so honest and yet so ugly, as raw hurt assembles itself on Ray's face.

"So I've lost you forever, then? Just like your mom." A single tear rolls down his cheek, and he swipes it away under the guise of adjusting his glasses.

My brows furrow. He's never shown any emotion like this before. Before I can react, he turns and storms out of the room. Speechless, I move to glance out the doorway and see him quickly stalking down the corridor. The truth is that I want to run after him, to explain everything, but I can't. He wouldn't understand, and this is my life now. The separation would have to be made at some point.

I glance at Bishop and Sam, who are for once dazed into silence. The realization hits me full force: I just traded my Dad for my team. Traded the little family I have for Wandering. I run to my room and slam the door, then toss myself on my bed, crying.

Two hearts ripped out in one day.

No

26

THE
TRUTH

THE GALA AND ACADEMY CLASSES ARE CAN-
celed for a week and a half. The building must be put
back together, the Relic Archives rebuilt, and some walls
reconstructed. Students are nursed back to health. Overall,
there's a quiet sadness. Rumors of the Underground spread
like wildfire. And finally, on Friday, we're called to an assembly to learn the truth.

Over a loudspeaker, Gabe summons students to the main
atrium. His voice is unusually solemn, but most of us have
been since the attack.

Bishop, Sam, and I crowd against the banister, looking down at the first floor. Macey shoves in with Xavier. Quinn hobbles on crutches next to them. Atticus has just been released from the hospital. Agnes and Scarlett, with her arm in a cast, settle nearby.

Some students sit on the main stairs like a stadium. Collectively, there's a low rumble of chatter. Whispers question what information the school administrators might reveal. I note that the noise would be louder if many of the conversations weren't taking place telepathically between some Protectors and Seers.

I'm nervous, anticipating the worst, for I know that the information we're about to hear can only be negative. I try to remain strong, but my anger has caused me many sleepless nights.

To combat them, I've spent every allowable second in the training room. Now that Bishop knows of my abilities, I haven't bothered to hide my training. Ms. Swift, thrilled with my eagerness to improve, works with me for hours on end.

Bishop drapes his arm around my back and rubs my shoulder. He squeezes me closer, brushing his lips to my hair. "You need sleep, love. You've been working too hard."

"It'll never be good enough."

He tenses at my response, so I know this *new me* upsets him. I sigh and lean into him, holding him tight. My affection is the only way I can assure him that I still need him, even if I probably don't need him as a Protector.

My eyes roam and notice Turner. He's on the first floor with his arms crossed, staring at me. He refused to stay at the hospital beyond a few days. He winces when he rotates his torso in certain ways; his stitches pulling, I'd guess. I've yet to talk to him, even to check on him, since I've promised myself to stay away as Sam suggested.

I wonder if he knows about the conversation I had with Hologram Turner. And I wonder if the conversation would have gone the same way with the real Turner. From the look on his face, I think so.

Perpetua makes her way next to him and whispers in his ear. I tense, seeing them together. She's been lying low since the attack, only appearing when she wants to remind me about the crystal. Everyone here knows about her team's involvement with the Underground, which hasn't made her very popular.

How long will she give me to look for the crystal before she tells Bishop about Turner and me? Tonight, I promise myself that no matter how difficult the conversation might be, I'll stop procrastinating, be strong, and explain myself to Bishop. I have nothing to hide. I've fought Turner's advances on many occasions. If anyone should feel guilty, it should be Turner.

Bishop squeezes me again, and I quickly avert my eyes.

Steel shades slide over the windows and click, locking into place. The lights dim. A hologram clicks on, appearing on the first floor below. It's a 3-D emblem, a shield with a coiled snake, ten feet high, rotating in the air. Presumably, this is the shield of the Underground. The light the image creates illuminates everyone's faces.

"Wanderers have never had a peaceful life. From the beginning of time, when we were placed on this earth, there has been much turmoil because with this amazing power of time travel comes infinite duty," Mr. Evanston's voice booms.

"The Underground Brotherhood of the Snake, or Underground, for short, was created for only one reason—to undermine the duties that we, as good Wandering Society citizens, have placed upon ourselves since our beginnings in Gibeon: knowledge, evolution, and co-existence.

"The Underground has done everything in its power to manipulate time and rotate its axis in favor of their ideals. It seems they're against everything the Society stands for and will stop at nothing until our kind has been wiped from this earth. By attempting to do so, on many sad occasions they've unintentionally set off an extremely dangerous domino effect—creating wars, plagues, famines, and other heinous events." The hologram image changes to quick images, representing each event.

"Many negotiation efforts have been made on behalf of the Society of Wanderers by Grand Master Phineas Levi to resolve this issue. Unfortunately, his endeavors have been met with resistance and with absolutely no peaceful resolution." Mr. Evanston steps away.

Terease walks over and joins in the presentation. "At this

moment, it's not completely clear what has instigated these new, vicious Underground attacks. I personally, with the help of our assigned Society agents, have been seeking them out, looking for answers," Terease says and gestures to a nearby group of Society soldiers.

"What I can assure you is that you are now safe." She paces. "Many of you have probably noticed increased security around the Academy. Professor Raunnebaum has initiated a new security system. He'll share information on that now." She gestures to the professor.

"Good afternoon, students." Professor Raunnebaum slides in front of the rotating hologram. "I've shipped in many new Animates to patrol the Academy and Olde Town areas. They'll be on the lookout for any unauthorized persons attempting to wander into the area."

A ghastly roar reverberates off the atrium walls. Two fire-breathing Animates fly over our heads, swoop across the room, and land with a loud clank next to Professor Raunnebaum. Their long, extended bodies undulate with machine-like precision, metal scraping upon metal, until they find a coiled position of rest.

"These Chinese dragons and many others are our new additions." Professor Raunnebaum strokes the scalloped gills of one Animate. Smoke coils from its nostrils, drifting away into the air.

"Now," Mr. Evanston says as he steps into view. "If anyone has any specific concerns, please see myself or any faculty member immediately." He glances around pointing to the group. "Because we've been through so much this week, Gabe would like to address you."

Gabe steps forward, more restrained than I have ever seen him, dressed somberly in black with his hands folded behind his back. "Hello, students. We realize how hard this week has been, so this evening, we would like for everyone to forget your worries and try to have a little fun. Yes, fun!" Gabe clasps his hands in front of his chest, igniting his normal bubbly personality. "Tonight, I'm very excited to announce that we'll be holding our gala ball!" He throws out his arms with exuberance.

The students cheer, clapping and whistling at the news. I can't help but smile. It would be nice to think about something other than revenge. I'm happy for a moment, and then remember that I've promised myself to talk to Bishop. *I will—tonight. No matter what.*

"I thought you might feel that way!" Gabe rips off his black attire, revealing his circus ringmaster costume. Red sparkles shimmer in a spotlight encircling him. The Underground snake emblem morphs into new hologram—a group of enthusiastic spider monkeys. One leaps to Gabe's shoulder. The others run off, squeaking and bouncing into the crowd.

"Garment bags have been delivered to your rooms with your gala costumes. Please meet here, tonight at eight!" Gabe spins as two cannons of glitter explode. Sparkles flutter through the air. Cheers grow louder as the students release their anxiety, nearly giddy with excitement.

The window shades release with a loud, simultaneous click and slide open, revealing the sunlight.

No

27

PROTECTORS

"PARDON ME," MACEY SAYS AND SQUEEZES BEtween Bishop and me. "I need to have some girl time with my B.F.F." She winks at him. Students rush to their apartments, pushing past.

"Of course." He nods and smiles. "I'd never dream of coming between you two." With a quick squeeze, he releases my arm, surrendering me to Macey.

"We'll catch ya later!" she hollers over her shoulder and marches into her apartment. "I have the whole day planned— you, me, and Jesus Holy-Hotness, my hair stylist."

"Mace, I'm supposed to be meeting Ms. Swift for defense

tutoring." I attempt to resist, half-heartedly pulling away from her. She tugs harder, dragging me into her bedroom and slams the door.

"Yeah, about that." She turns and looks serious. "What's with all this anger you've been releasing in girl-kick-butt mode? Scarlett said you practically ripped her arm off in defense class the other week. If you're going to be Rambo Barbie, at least take it out on Perpetua."

"Yeah, sorry. I guess I got a little carried away. I apologized to her right away."

"Scarlett's fine. That's not why I mentioned it." She shakes her head. "It's just—" She hesitates, letting her eyes roam nervously.

"Tell me."

She sighs and gives in. "I see what you're doing to Bishop. You're kinda hurting his feelings." She plops on her bed, looking guilty for the accusation.

"He said that to you?" My heart races, and I cross my arms, wishing I could strangle this ridiculous urge to fight out of my system.

"He doesn't have to. I know how'd I'd feel it you were my Wanderer. I think—no, I *know*, it would make me self-conscious. Like, I know it shouldn't, but in my heart, in my genetics, I know it would." She looks uncomfortable.

I've never seen Macey like this. "Don't be afraid. You can tell me what you think. I want to know." I place a hand on her shoulder.

"It's just upsetting to even think about." Macey shakes her head. "Like, providing protection is who I am. If Xavier could do it for himself, what good am I?" She scrunches her nose. "Maybe it's a stupid Wandering thing?"

"You're right." I collapse on the bed next to her. Professor Raunnebaum warned me of this, and I moved forward with my training regardless, knowing it would affect Bishop. "I've been feeling insanely guilty about it, knowing it would throw off the balance of our team, but for some reason, I can't stop." All Underground and mom issues aside, I think I still might be doing this. Like, it's the path I'm meant to be on.

"All right, well, I'll get off my soapbox now. It's your team. And considering the attack, it's always good to have another fighter." She gives me a hug.

"You can always tell me how you feel, Mace. Okay?"

She nods with a smile.

It's time to discuss everything with Bishop, not just the Turner issue. I sigh.

"Now, let's talk about something fun, like hair and makeup for the gala." Macey squeals and runs to grab her makeup box.

•

I cancel my tutoring with Ms. Swift. And after a visit to Jesus, the miracle hairdresser, Macey and I have the most beautiful hairstyles you can imagine. My hair is pulled back in the front and layered in long dark ringlets down the center of my back. Because I feel like letting loose, I allow Jesus to add a small streak of sapphire blue to my hair. Somewhere between my night classes,

I dreamed about having the color. Amazingly, it matches beautifully with the dress Gabe left for me.

The dress shimmers with the color of sapphire. Emerald-green details line the edges. There's a fascinator hairpiece with long, curling peacock feathers and sparkling cobalt gems. The costume is a mixture of steampunk style and Victorian circus. The black fishnet stockings are sexy but a little too itchy. Macey promises I'll get used to them as I yank and tug at them.

There's a knock at Macey's apartment front door. Xavier, dressed in a brown suit, hurries to answer it. Bishop stands with Sam on his arm. The second she sees me, she sweeps into the room in a panic.

"Do you see this dress?" She sticks her long leg out of a slit in her skirt that ends at her hip, right above her panties. "It's ridiculous! Too much! How am I supposed to go to this party looking like a floozy, Sera? Why would Gabe do this to me?" she hisses with a dramatic stomp.

"I kinda like it." Quinn stands nearby, his weight leaning on his crutches.

Sam steps aside, holding her leg out. "It's absurd, Quinn!"

"Not with stems like those," he responds, wagging his eyebrows playfully.

Sam instantly blushes, becoming quiet. Her gaze drifts, looking for a comfortable place to land.

"It's not too bad," I venture, trying to ease her distress. "At least your ruffled briefs are cute." I smile behind my glove.

Sam sighs and crosses her arms.

"You look lovely, Sam," Bishop says, patting her shoulder in a brotherly fashion. And then he turns. "As do you, Miss Parrish." He grabs my hand and kisses the base of my fingers.

"So do you." His sapphire-blue ascot, tufted under his chin, strangely matches with my new streak of hair color, like Gabe knew I would do it. When I look into Bishop's eyes, I'm feeling more confident in the conversation I'll be having with him tonight. *I have nothing to hide.* I smile brightly, feeling happy for the love we share. I lean in and kiss him on the cheek.

Bishop takes my arm and, as a group, we head to the main atrium. A hologram has completely transformed the space. Now, it's the grandest ballroom one could imagine with the most ornate details. Bright gold leaf carvings and paintings cover every available flat surface. Rows of columns and arcades run along the outer edges of the first and second floor. Red-and-white-striped curtains drape and billow on every wall, mimicking the tent of a circus. Holographic circus animals roam the floor, adorned with ornate gold cords, gemstones, and feathers.

But most amazing by far is the sight of miniature hot air balloons that hover at various heights. Their baskets are just large enough for two people. Some balloons rise higher than the ceiling, which now appears to open up to the midnight blue sky. Holographic stars twinkle. A shimmering comet streaks across the atmosphere.

"Wow!" Xavier says. "Turner really outdid himself."

"Turner?" Macey questions.

"Yeah, he's an amazing artist. He designed the whole ballroom for Gabe. Said he wanted to impress some girl," he snorts. I can't help it, I stop breathing, knowing *that girl* is me. As hard as I try to kick Turner out of my head, he keeps fighting his way back in.

"Look, there he is." Xavier points.

I follow his finger. Perpetua wraps herself around Turner's body and kisses his neck. He doesn't seem responsive, but still, he's doing what I told him to do, finding someone else. Why does it have to be her? I grit my teeth.

"Guess it worked." Macey laughs. "Never knew those two were an item. He's got awful taste. Did you know, Sera?" She looks over, completely clueless about my non-feelings for him.

"No." I shake my head. My body temperature rises.

By the time we make it to the lower level, the music has taken on a club vibe. Students migrate to the floor, swaying and spinning to some kind of modern techno mixed with a carnival waltz. Bishop immediately sweeps me onto the dance floor. The moves are easy to pick up and, in no time, we've learned the choreographed steps.

He spins me in between the clowns and stilt-walkers. But I can't enjoy myself with Perpetua hanging on Turner in my peripheral vision. I grab Bishop's hand and lead him to a hot air balloon.

A gypsy approaches. Wiry salt-and-pepper hair peeks out from under an eggplant-colored hooded cape. Many reflective necklaces dangle from her neck. Hypnotically, they clank and chime when she moves. Once upon a time, she was probably very beautiful. She stops and points with her knobby finger.

"Are you prepared to see your future, young one?"

"My future?"

"The balloon." She looks up at its decorative exterior, draped with roped nets and tassels. "To ride in it, to see above the walls of the ballroom, will reveal your future like a crystal ball."

"Sounds like fun," I muse. These are only circus games, holograms thrown together by Gabe and Turner.

"You are a brave one," she says, waddling aside to pull open the basket gate. Two students step out and Bishop and I step in. The gypsy closes the gate, then ambles around the basket and unties a gold cord tethered to it, releasing the balloon. It ascends, launching into the air. The basket's edges are high, at chest level, so Bishop and I lean over to look over at the party below.

"I should be scared of the height, but for some reason I'm not. Maybe it's because my mind knows it's a hologram."

"Maybe, but still, you shouldn't be afraid. I've never understood your fear of heights. Perhaps you're finally getting over it?"

"I wish!" I laugh at the thought, but for once, I'm thrilled to be leaving the nerves behind, even for a fake hot air balloon ride. "Look, we're rising higher than the roofline." I point.

"What do you think you'll see?" Bishop questions. "It's a peek into your future. Maybe *our* future?" He lifts one eyebrow and places his hand on mine.

Bishop reaches above us and activates the burner. The burner's flame roars, creating hot air that rises into the balloon, and we float higher. "Let's see how far we can go. Maybe to heaven?"

He flashes his dimple.

"Maybe," I tease.

The balloon ascends beyond the roofline of the Academy. I'm amazed by what's revealed below. It's not the bustling city of Chicago as I expected.

•

The skyline of a quiet desert surrounds us. Stars reach across the convex sky, their light softly touching the undulating, sand-covered land below. The moon reflects upon a shimmering river that cuts the earth in half. Structures, Egyptian in style, sit beyond. Fireflies dance at a golden obelisk's base. If we floated toward it, I could reach out and touch the apex.

"How is this possible?" I turn to Bishop. "How can my future be the desert? And I've dreamed of this before, long ago—the night Aunt Mona told me I'm a Wanderer." I gesture toward the sky, thinking back to the dream about fireflies in the desert.

"It's beautiful, whatever it means." His arms encircle my waist. "Any place in time is my favorite place to be with you. If this is your future, I want to be there with you." He brushes his nose against my cheek. His warm breath radiates heat along my bare shoulder. And finally, his lips find mine. His kisses are sweet, controlled, and soft.

Gently, I push him away. "Bishop, there's something I want to talk to you about. Totally not a big deal." Ashamed, I look down, knowing it's a complete lie. It'll be a big deal to Bishop.

"Then let's chat about it later," he persuades, kissing me again.

№ 28

THE GALA

T HE BALLOON LANDS. WE'VE FLOWN ABOVE
the party for at least half an hour, maybe more. I didn't
get a chance to talk with Bishop, but I haven't broken my
promise to myself. The evening isn't over. Tonight, after the
party, we *will* talk.

Lights flash above. Gabe appears at the top of a grand
staircase, dressed in a costume, this one slightly more cabaret
than the others. He wears red heels, black fishnets, and a tux
with tails. A large black top hat with feathers, crinkled tulle,
and a mound of flowers, stacks high on his head. Black kohl
wraps his eyes like a raccoon, and his face is caked with white

powder. As always, he's stunning, no matter what form he takes. Still, this outfit, without sequins, is bland compared to his others. In his own way, he's mourning the attack.

"Hello, my little carnies!" He steps down slowly, leaning on a red cane. "The festivities have begun. Let's have some entertainment, shall we?" The lights snap off, save for one spotlight. The beam rotates to Gabe and then splits into several. Each new light lands on the hot air balloons above. At first, the balloons sizzle. Then, with a confetti explosion, the fabric peels back like the skin of an orange, revealing large silver hoops. Women—or men, in some cases I can't tell— stand in them, dressed like Gabe, balancing on the ring.

Music fills the ballroom, dance and orchestra in a perfect blend. As each dramatic note hits, the acrobats standing in their silver hoops strike new poses. Finally, the music breaks into full chorus, and the group performs an aerial choreographed dance of acrobatics.

One performer does a handstand with legs stretched in splits long and wide. In another, two people twine themselves into an impossible position, one balancing on the other within their own spinning ring. Several acrobats flip and jump between other swinging circles like trapeze artists. There's so much taking place, it's hard to focus on just one.

At the culmination of the music, the troupe rolls over the side of their rings, flipping into the air and disappearing within several sparkling clouds of wander dust. The crowd cheers wildly, but Gabe's not done yet. The show continues for at least another hour. Funny and scary clowns, mermaids swimming around ornate fish tanks, tattooed lizard men spitting fire, acrobats riding colorful horses, dancing tigers, there's nothing this circus doesn't have. Each act is more devastatingly shocking and beautiful than the last.

When it stops, I can barely catch my breath. Students clap and scream and whistle for more, but the show is apparently over. Eventually the DJ returns to spinning music, and students return to dancing. A large buffet has been set out in a nearby room.

"Would you like some food?" Bishop asks after another dance. "I'm starving."

"Sounds good."

Bishop makes his way through the crowd, disappearing from view. Now, I finally have a moment to do what I've wanted to do this whole night. I scan the crowd. When I find Turner alone I march to him, where he's pouring punch for himself. Perpetua chats with a group of friends across the room.

I stand next to him, practically boiling out of my skin. With quick movements, I grab a cup, swipe the ladle from his grasp, and pour a drink for myself. I take a quick swig, casting my disapproving eyes from behind the rim, and then I slam the glass on the table. My opinion can't be held in any longer.

"I can't believe you brought her with you!"

"Are you suggesting you have a problem with my date?" He smiles, acting innocent.

"She's a horrid, back-stabbing witch!"

He shoves an arm under mine and hisses, "Aren't you the one who told me to move on, Seraphina? What was it you said exactly? 'Find someone new,' I think it was." He drags me out a set of ornate doors and onto a veranda that overlooks a holographic city. Turner kicks the doors closed behind us. The party and music disappear, leaving us in silence.

"Uh!" I grunt and stomp away, but he latches onto my arm.

"No! We're having this out now! You aren't going any-where!" He swings me back to face him. "Why don't you ask yourself why you're so jealous of her?"

"Jealous! I am not!" I scream. "You're out of your delu-sional mind!" I pull away.

But he isn't done with me. He pulls me back again. My body lands with my chest against his. Before I can react or even say another word, he crushes his lips into mine and kisses me. I struggle to get away, but he holds me there, let-ting his hungry fingers skim over my shoulders and down my back. His kisses are frantic, hot, and out of control. I lose my mind, because suddenly, I kiss him back.

All the tension that has built up between us explodes into fireworks. They sizzle through my veins, shooting throughout my body. The kiss, heated with passion, is the consequence of the raw and careless emotional disturbance that's been build-ing for months. His scorching lips work mine over. I reach into his dark hair and twine my fingers into its roots, pulling him closer, gasping for more.

Turner kisses the line of my collarbone and bare shoulders. In the frenzy, he lifts me from the floor and staggers backward. I land seated on a ledge and lock my legs around his hips. Then I grab his collar, jerk him closer, and vanish into absolute delirium. There's passion—so much more intense passion than I've ever felt before.

"Sera!" The veranda doors fly open.

We pull away from each other. Turner's wistful eyes lock with mine. I drag my wrist across my wet lips, breathing heavily. I want to jump back into his arms and devour him when he steps away.

Sam rushes forward. Her beautiful taffeta gown sweeps behind her. She slaps Turner in the face and grabs my arm, quickly dragging me away. I only look back over my shoulder, staring at his silvery eyes. I want to return and allow his kisses to consume me. A ghost of a smirk reaches his lips as though he can read my mind. Then he's gone from my view.

Inside, Sam drags me through the people dancing, holographic animals, jugglers, and finally out a door on the opposite side of the grand ballroom. She shoves me into the ladies room, drags me to a circular sofa, and pushes me down on the seat.

"Sit!" she commands, but she doesn't have to. Lost in this abyss of complete and utter shock, I would have let her guide me anywhere. My stunned mind buzzes as I stare off into space. A single finger lingers at my lips, brushing the exact spot where I just allowed Turner to kiss me in a way I never dreamed imaginable.

A set of fingers snaps in front of my eyes, awakening me. Sam paces back and forth, biting her nails. *She never bites her nails.*

Awareness drenches me. "Don't tell Bishop!" I plead. "Don't let him see into your mind or show him what you saw!" The words tumble from my lips at a hurried, frantic pace. "Please!" I jump up and grab her arm, imploring with desperate eyes as my fingers dig into her skin.

Fear surges through me when she doesn't answer. "I don't know what happened. He just—kissed me, and I fought, but then I didn't." I stare off again, considering the awful consequences of my actions. Overwhelmed, I fall to the floor. My gown puddles around me. I lean into the billowing fabric and cry.

Sam bends down, bringing her eyes level with mine. Her mouth turns down at the corners. "Sera," she says gently, her eyes brimming with tears. "Bishop's already seen."

№

29

ONE KISS

HEARTBREAK. I ACTUALLY HEAR MY HEART BREAK. It shakes and crushes into a thousand little pieces that seep out of my body. They float away into the air, extinguishing into nothing. I feel nothing; I am nothing.

Sam wraps her arm around my back, helping me to stand. She enlists someone else to help. I hear the exchange, but it doesn't completely register. I don't even bother to see who it is, or care to recognize the voice. I want to disappear into my sadness, allow my body to fold up into nothing. *Bishop knows. He saw me kiss Turner through Sam's mind. What have I done?*

·

When I begin to come to my senses, I realize we're on the catwalk of the ballroom, sitting on a bench, looking down at the gala. People are twirling and dancing to music I don't hear.

"Sera, can you hear me?" A sad voice breaks through.

I tilt my head listlessly; my eyes land on Sam.

"Pay attention if you can," she says. "I have a lot to tell you, and I'm sorry it has to be now."

My brows furrow. There's not much life in me.

"Look around, do you see everyone dancing down there?" Sam asks and gestures toward the crowd. I sluggishly turn my head in the direction of the fun. "Do you see Macey, Quinn, and Xavier?"

I nod.

"Now, do you see Jessica and Stu? Or Agnes and Atticus? Do you notice anything they have in common?"

"No," I whimper.

"They're dating…they're in love."

"So?"

"Think about it. They're all in teams. Remember the connection we had when we first met? For me, I knew you were my family, and I'd never even met you before. In my heart, I knew you belonged to me," Sam explains.

"Yes, I remember the feeling," I mumble.

"Now think of Bishop. The first time you saw him, how you felt—that attraction, an unreasonable attraction beyond teenage hormones. You wanted him even though you had no idea who he was."

"What are you saying?"

"I'm saying, Sera, that it doesn't matter that you kissed Turner. Bishop will forgive you. He doesn't have a choice. He *has* to love you."

"What?" I sit up a little.

"I'm saying, we as a team of Wanderers, Seers, and Protectors are genetically predisposed to love one another. We are our own best matches, soul mates."

"You're saying I don't have a choice who I love?"

"Well, actually, you have a choice. Unlike others, you have a very unique choice—one that was never given to you. You had a choice to love one of two people, a choice most of us don't get. And the choice was stolen from you."

"Sam, you're not making any sense."

"You have two Protectors, Sera. Or you did before you came to the Academy."

It clicks immediately. Turner doesn't have a team. "I suppose you could say it just didn't work out," he said when I asked him about them. I assumed that meant they didn't take the oaths and decided to live as Normals.

"How?"

"Twins, Sera. Both meant for you. Only one can have your love. Only one can be our Protector."

"Who—who decided for me?"

She clears her throat. "I promised I would never tell, but I can't stand to see you like this. It's not fair, and you deserve to know." She grabs my hand and tightens her fingers around mine. "The moment Bishop saved you from the gang in the metro last year, the moment you talked to him in the Academy courtyard, it was decided for you. Bishop kinda—cheated."

"Cheated?"

"He and Turner were told to wait, not to reveal themselves to you. Terease was to administer some kind of test to see who you gravitated toward. The one you chose would have been our Protector, the one you would love forever. And I'm starting to think, it may not have been Bishop." She frowns.

"What about you, how come you didn't choose?"

"I was too young at the time. I didn't connect with either in that romantic way. I only saw them as my brothers, equally suited for the job, and I still do, because they're both in love with you. My match will be made with an odd member of another team."

I let it sink in, remembering every instance Bishop popped up when I moved to Chicago, every strange emotion I felt when I was compelled to be near him, stare at him, talk to him. I never thought I didn't have a choice. Why didn't I question how irrational everything was?

"He sent me his photograph," I say.

"What?"

"Before I moved here, when my wandering abilities started appearing in Miami, I received an envelope. It had Bishop's photo in it. It must have been him, trying to seal his own fate." I glance at her.

Sam's expression reflects her horror. "I—I can't believe it." She frowns with obvious disappointment.

"Me neither." I'm sad. I'm mad. I'm confused. If I were feeling more like myself, I'd want to lash out, make someone pay. Not for taking away my choice between two boys, but for taking away my choice, period. I was delusional to think that my relationship with Bishop was pure, untouched by the laws of Wandering. Nothing seems immune.

"There's more." She clears her throat.

"Please, no. This is bad enough." I sink back and hug my stomach, holding myself together. I might split apart at the seams if I let go.

"We have to leave for me to explain. You'll have to see it for yourself."

Nº

30

AN ARRANGEMENT

S AM AND I LEAVE THE GALA. SHE DRAGS ME
through the empty corridors to our apartment. I'm ap-
prehensive. "Is Bishop here?" I'm not ready to see him. I don't
even know what I'll say to him, how to feel.

"No, don't worry."

She walks into my bedroom and heads for the closet. She
pulls out the first outfit she sees—the one hanging on the
door—and throws it at me. "You'll need to change. You're
going to wander."

"In this?" I look at the outfit, the one I saw myself wearing
in London that day, weeks ago.

"It's as good as anything else." She shrugs.

She doesn't know the significance of the outfit. I sigh. Sam leaves my room as I change. I shimmy out of my costume, letting everything fall to the floor. I step into a pair of gray leggings, a skirt, t-shirt, and suede jacket.

On my desk sits my oath package. I unlock it, lift the top, and remove my new phone. I shove it in my pocket when Sam returns with a relic.

"Here." She drops a set of keys into my palm.

"These are Bishop's house keys." I turn them over, considering why she'd want me to wander with them.

"You must go there to see, and you have to leave now, before anyone finds out what I've done."

"Just tell me, please."

"Trust me, Sera. If I had known what I know now, I would have told you so much sooner. You need to see it for yourself."

"Fine."

We climb out Sam's window and down the leafy vines that wind around the walls of the Academy's facade. Society soldiers dressed in plain clothes stand at the entrance, but they seem more worried about who wants to come in, rather than which students are sneaking out.

There's a crisp autumn chill in the air. I pull my jacket closed as Sam and I make our way to the center of the courtyard, next to the obelisk. Only the city continues to move. Taxis and cars fly past the nearest streets. All the others in the school, including the teachers, are still enjoying the festivities.

"Do you have the relic?"

"Yes." I hold up Bishop's keys.

"You'll repeat this as your keyword to travel to London: 'August, twenty-five, this year, three o'clock.'"

She's just confirmed what I know is coming, I'm going to London, the day I visited Bishop over summer vacation. I nod, a little sad for the tears I know are coming. There's a good possibility my life will get worse, but how, I can't even comprehend.

"August, twenty-five, this year, three o'clock." I say the keywords out loud and grasp the keys. Then I say the phrase in my mind, letting the numbers swirl through my head, injecting them into my soul. I bolt, leaving Sam behind as I run across the courtyard, feet pounding the grass. I pump my arms, pushing them farther, until I hear the familiar rumble. The ground shakes, buildings crack in half, grass rips, the city rolls up into the sky behind me like a carpet, blocking the twinkling stars and the breeze off Lake Michigan. The land finally races down from the sky and slams me into a time-traveling wormhole.

I launch feet first into inky nothingness. Colors of the night swirl and ripple, increasing into light. My feet land on firm ground in a running stop. Cobblestone streets wrap around a neighborhood of Victorian homes and flats. This is Chelsea, London. Bishop's home stands fifty feet away. With shaky determination, I walk to the front door.

Instead of using the keys, I knock on the door. If Bishop

answers, he'll have no knowledge that I've betrayed him to Turner yet. Where I am in time now is weeks before that event ever takes place. I relax my shoulders and try not to appear guilty, not to appear as though I know our love has been tainted.

The door creaks open. Thirteen-year-old Charlotte, Bishop and Turner's little sister, stands at the door. Her face, fresh with youth, sparkles pretty as a peach. Her strawberry-blonde hair hangs to her shoulders, and her eyes shine with recognition, even though I have never met her before.

"Sera!" She giggles with delight and pulls me into a hug. "However did you get here?" She squeals and drags me down the hall. Bishop told me that she's a Normal and so far she hasn't shown signs of becoming a Wanderer. She doesn't know how lucky she is.

"Oh, I was just in the neighborhood." I make a joke. It's the easiest way.

"Mum," she calls. "You aren't going to believe who's here!" She drags me into the main living area.

"Who, darling?"

I stop in my tracks when I see Aunt Mona standing at the kitchen counter, cutting carrots. Mona looks up, her face draining of blood as her eyes meet mine, and she slices her finger with the knife. Apparently she's as surprised as I am. I spin around, looking for anyone else in the room, but there's only Mona.

"Oh, blast!" She holds up one finger, beginning to drip

blood, and sticks it in her mouth.

"Mum, are you all right?" Charlotte runs to her aid.

"Yes, but why don't you run and fetch me a plaster from the medical," she says in an unfamiliar British accent.

Charlotte runs off on her errand. I'm thankful she doesn't see my face as she leaves.

When the sound of her steps disappear up the stairs, I turn to Mona and hiss, "What the hell is going on, Mona? Why is Charlotte calling you 'Mom'?" A tear escapes.

Mona frantically sweeps forward, ready to gather me into a hug. Is she really going to try to console me? I lunge away from her, too angry to let her touch me. I back up to a nearby wall, to keep a safe distance.

"Sera, oh, I knew this day would come, but I didn't know it would be here so quickly. Who told you? How did you know?"

"I didn't." My lips tremble. Somehow Sam knew. She wanted me to see. Mona is Bishop and Turner's mom.

"How? Please tell me Bishop is not my cousin," I blurt, gripping my stomach to hold in the disgust that roils there.

"No, of course not!" She takes off her apron and tosses it on the counter. She sighs and holds her hand to her head, massaging the skin as though she has a headache.

Charlotte returns. "Here ya go." She hands Mona a bandage and lingers nearby.

"Love," Mona says to Charlotte, "I'd like very much to talk with Sera, alone. Do you think you could leave for a bit?"

"But—but—that's not fair," she whines. "I want to talk with her too. I want to hear about the States." She pouts and crosses her arms.

"How about we ask Sera to stay for dinner and you can question her to death then?" She runs a hand through the girl's hair and pinches her chin lovingly.

"All right," Charlotte concedes and runs off, up the stairs. Mona sighs and turns her gaze back to me. "Sorry, she's wanted nothing more than to meet you with Bishop talking about you all the time, showing her pictures of you. I think she's a little jealous of the boys going to the Academy in the States." She gives me a strained smile.

I don't even know how to look at Mona, what to say, what to do. I want to run away and never see her face again. I want to lash out and make her hurt as much as I do. But all I can do is stand here, too stunned to react.

"Why don't we sit?" Mona gestures to the sofa and chair. This house is different, not decorated in the usual eclectic Mona way. It's Normal. I waver, unsure about what to do. Stay or go? Cry or fight?

Mona slips past and sits. I stay put, plastered against the wall, still undecided on how to react.

"As a mother, I had to make a difficult decision a very long time ago," she starts, staring out the window. "The boys weren't even born yet, but I knew I was having twins. I kept it a secret for as long as I could, hoping there would be some way to save both of them." She looks over, her eyes wavering.

Her hands twist in her lap, the way they always do when she's nervous. "So, when the Society came for my babies, for one of them, I made a deal."

"What—what do you mean, 'came for one of them'?" I ask, voice trembling.

"Twins, Sera, are not sanctioned by Society laws. One must die to ensure the seamless life of a Wanderer for the other. Two Protectors on one team cannot exist without consequences."

"They'd kill one of them?"

"Yes."

"That's ridiculous! How would they even know as babies that they'd turn? They could have been Normal!"

"True, but the Society doesn't function under possible unknowns. They like everything very neatly tied up. And it's been this way for thousands of years."

I can't even fathom that what she's saying is real. *Who could kill a baby?*

"What was the deal you made to save them?" I croak. I don't even want to know what awful thing they'd force her do to save her children. After the last hour, I hate everything about the Society.

"At the time, I told them I'd do anything. They agreed to spare the twins but told me they would come back when they needed help. And whenever and whatever that was, I could not refuse.

"Naturally, I was scared of what they would want. The

thought terrified me for months. I hoped it would be years before they came back, but the boys were very young when the Society returned. Your mother had just passed away, and the only thing they requested was that I play the part of your aunt."

I want to say, "Mom didn't die, Mona," but I keep the truth hidden. At this moment, I don't trust anyone anymore. Everything that I've forced myself to believe all of my life is crumbling into nothing.

Mona continues. "Back then, it seemed such a simple request for saving one of my boys. With your father being a Normal, the Society simply wanted me to watch over you on occasion. I did it without hesitation, never considering that it might somehow hurt you. Acting as your aunt was an easy transition because your mom had always introduced me as her sister. She'd even introduced me as her sister to your father long ago. It was the easiest way to explain our close relationship to the Normals. You see—your mom was my Wanderer."

"*Your* Wanderer? You told me a girl named Ann was your wanderer!"

"Yes, *Eliza* Ann."

Ann—my mom's middle name. Mona had told me as much as she could without giving too much away.

"There's so much more that I can't even tell you. I'm so sorry I deceived you, Sera." Mona glances at me, tears in her eyes. Her mouth pulls into a frown. "Nothing's changed. I still love you as though you're one of my own children." She stands and reaches for me.

I step away, just out of her reach. I want to believe her, but right now I can't believe anyone.

The front door unlocks, creaking open. I turn to see who's come home. Bishop's dad, maybe? Mona's husband? I can't even imagine who it'll be next.

No. 31

UNRAVEL

I HEAR HIS VOICE BEFORE I SEE HIM. BUT IT'S
not Bishop's voice that makes me stiffen; it's Perpetua's.

"Do you think it'll work?" she asks him.

"Yes, I believe it might be the key for all of us," Bishop responds.

I look around the corner and see the two standing at the door, facing each other, gazing into Perpetua's palm. They're inspecting something.

My heart stops, seeing them so close, so obviously friendly. The emptiness inside me sucks into a pit, a black hole, which nearly causes me to choke with suffocation.

They don't look up until I've descended on them. I'm so angry; I swipe what's in Perpetua's hand, stealing the object. Pushing between them, I run out the front door, descend the stairs, and around the corner. Bishop's house disappears, and I speed down the cobblestone street, zigzagging across many side roads.

Bishop and Perpetua chase, falling into step behind me. In many places, they appear out of nowhere as though they're impossibly popping in and out of time. They call my name, begging me to stop, but I ignore them. When I find a busy street of people, I launch in, disappearing in the madness.

Hours later, after I've lost them, I duck into an alley and lean against a brick wall. I'm crying, I'm sweating from running, and I'm an emotional mess. Tears fall until there's nothing left in my system. Emptiness. I have no choice who I love, who I am, who my extended family is, and now with everything that Bishop's done, I find him with Perpetua. I just can't take any more. I hate the Society and everything that my life has become.

I open my hand, revealing what I've stolen. Pricks of blood dot my skin from holding the crystal's jagged edges too tightly. This is the crystal that Perpetua accused me of taking. I don't know what it is, why it's so important, or even why I took it in the first place. Jealousy, probably. I wanted to hurt her for hurting me. The rock means something to Bishop too, and by taking it, I've somehow hurt him.

I turn it over. It vaguely reminds me of some crystal rocks

I saw in Professor Raunnebaum's laboratory, but I never asked what they were. I tuck it into my pocket and decide to keep moving. If I stay, Bishop and Perpetua will certainly find me.

I wander the streets of downtown London for another hour, just thinking. Thinking of everything that's wrong with my life: the way the Society manipulates us, how they take everything and pretend to give us the world. But they don't give you the things that matter—truth and love. They create a life for you and manipulate it, nurture the lies, and shove them down your throat. For weeks I'd been beating myself up, trying to protect Bishop from the knowledge of Turner flirting with me, from my advanced fighting abilities, and from meeting Cece again. All the while, he's had his own secrets—many of them.

"Bishop!" I hear someone call. At first I duck behind a crowd of people, certain that he and Perpetua have found me, but then I hear the voice again.

"Bishop!" I turn my head. It's me—the *old me*. I've collided with my past self, the one who came here weeks ago during summer vacation to find Bishop with the love letter relic. The old me stands, hoisted on a clock tower, the one that looks like a miniature version of Big Ben.

When she spots me, I see the recognition in her eyes, but I guess I shouldn't be surprised. Everything is playing out exactly the way it did before.

Confused, I run across a street. Cabbies scream past, barely missing me by inches. Something in my gut tells me to get away. I head in the direction everyone's moving. Victoria Station sits just ahead. I weave through the people, squeezing into the front doors. I linger, surveying all the directions I can run and hide.

The old me appears in the door. I run. She follows, mirroring my actions, several seconds behind.

I head toward the trains, going underground. When I jump on the tube, she rushes in on the opposite side of the car. Maybe I should confront myself? Explain all that's happened. *No. I can't. Not yet.* I think of what's coming for her today, her last perfect date with Bishop. I'm too selfish to alter the memory, even with how upset I am with him.

The train bobbles through a few stops, and I jump out at the Embankment station. My old me follows. That's when I take out my new cell phone and make a quick call to Bishop's cell.

"Cleopatra's Needle," I say into the phone when he answers.

"Sera! What number is this? Wait there. I'm coming!"

I hang up before he says any more.

I lead the old me to the waterfront. I step onto the Cleopatra's Needle monument, then turn and lean against the base. I inspect the crystal while I'm waiting for my old self to appear. I consider tossing it into the Thames River, letting it sink and wash away with the murky green water. I extend my arm, preparing to hurl it through the air, but I stop myself right before it leaves my hand. I'm too curious to let it go. It means something, and I have to find out what. I sit down and turn it over in my hands. The tears start again. I can't help myself.

"Sera!" Bishop yells. I look up. My old self has appeared. She turns and looks behind her. Bishop stands, staring at her. His eyes drift to me. I see he quickly understands what's happened. One girl is his present Sera and the other is his future Sera.

The old me runs and pulls him into an embrace. They melt into each other. She's so happy. I want to be that naive girl again. Somehow, I envy her.

Stepping around the obelisk, I peek around the corner as they embrace. His eyes rise to mine, lingering on my sad, tear-soaked face. His expression says it all. He's sorry.

I nod, but not as an acceptance of an apology, just as recognition that he knows he's in the wrong. The two lovers embracing will move on from their moment as though nothing's happened. They'll have a few wonderful nights together and then in a few weeks their world will turn into contrived crap.

There's enough room to run along the Thames and wander back home to Sam. It seems she's the only one I can trust now.

No

32

DREAMDRIVE

"HOW LONG HAVE YOU KNOWN?" I ASK SAM AS I walk into her bedroom and shut the door. I'm back on true time at the Academy.

"I've been piecing it together since the dinner with your family," she says, looking up from her cello. The music stops, and she gracefully rises and places the instrument on a stand in the corner. She turns and gives me a hug. "I'm so sorry," she whispers in my ear.

"How did you know?"

"I saw Mona in Bishop's mind when we were at dinner with your dad. He couldn't help but reminisce about family memories. He really misses her. And I know he's had a heavy heart for not being able to share it with you. He's been forbidden, given the circumstances. Not long after I pieced it together, I confronted him." She steps away and sits on the edge of the bed, her long legs sweeping out in front of her.

"Why didn't you tell me sooner?"

"He made me promise. And it's not like he doesn't love you Sera, he does. So does Mona. Of course, I can see the truth in his mind. You must never let on to the Society that you know—not ever. Who knows what they're capable of doing to them?" She stands and paces, clearly upset by the thought.

"Then he told you about Mona's deal to keep him and Turner safe?"

She nods and looks away.

"It's not right, Sam—what they're doing. The Society's manipulated my whole life, Mona's life, all our lives! How are we supposed to know what's real now? Will anything ever be?" We sit on the bed. I'm weary and drained of energy.

"How was London?" she asks, changing the subject.

"About as wonderful as you would expect." Then I have a thought. I pull out the crystal and hold it in my palm. "So, what's the deal with this? Any ideas?"

Sam stiffens. "Is this Perpetua's?"

"Bingo."

"You took this from her in London?" She scrunches her face.

"What?" *Oh crap, there's more.*

"Remember how you made me promise not to tell anyone about your mom being alive?" She grits her teeth.

I nod, not exactly sure where this is going.

"I kept my promise, kind of."

"Sam!"

"I tried, I really did. In fact, I never said anything. Bishop saw it in my mind! I'm so sorry, Sera. It was a few weeks after the incident. Please don't hate me, I couldn't help but think about it. And Bishop just showed up in my mind one day when I did."

"And?"

"Well, he's kind of been looking for her all these months."

"What?"

"Bishop's been doing it for you. He would do anything for you, Sera." She grabs my hand.

There's a spark of happiness that I can't exactly explain. Bishop's been helping me look for my mom in his own way, all this time. But then I realize my happiness is fake. My love for Bishop is not real; it's a fabricated lie.

Sam starts again. "Bishop sought out Perpetua's help. Through Terease he arranged an exchange for Perpetua and her team's return to the Academy for information on Cece and the Underground's whereabouts—"

"Which would lead to my mom!"

"Exactly," Sam nods. "I think this crystal was part of the trade. Perpetua took it from Cece, hoping it would act as a bargaining chip to come back to school. She needed to convince Terease she was worthy. Ever since you took the crystal, Perpetua's been looking for it. She wouldn't be able to stay at the Academy without the trade. Terease gave her a deadline to find it. That's why she's been on your case."

"How long have you known about that?" I glance at her.

"Not long. They wanted to try to keep you out of it, to stop you before you took the crystal, but they didn't know when you were going to steal it. I guess we know now."

"Why didn't they just send someone to get it?"

"They tried. Apparently a million times, but the timing was never right. Except once. Perpetua fought you for it. The night you hurt your back."

I gasp. "That was *her*?" I think back to that rainy night in London when Bishop and I were attacked. "That witch, I should have known she would rip my skin off for it. She attacked the wrong me! I didn't have the crystal yet. Stupid girl!"

I shake off my anger and refocus on the matter at hand.

"What is it?" I wonder out loud, as I hold the crystal to the light.

"I think it's a hard drive for a contrapulator. Turns out that the Society not only makes us listen to classes at night, but they steal our dreams, too. They're stored on something just like this." She points to the crystal.

I jump up and head for Sam's contrapulator. Just like mine, the machine sits on her bedside table. The mishmash of metal components resembles a clock that's been flipped inside out. When turned on, a black screen shows green brain waves that jump and ripple.

I tip the machine forward and sure enough, there's a crystal inserted into the back, just like a removable hard drive. I tug on it. It clicks, slowly releasing. I shouldn't be surprised that this machine does more than it appears to. Holding both crystals, I compare the two.

Sam joins me. "Perpetua's crystal is larger. A little different, but this certainly must be the same thing. Maybe I should meditate on it?" she asks.

"Yes, that's a good idea." I hand her both.

Sam settles on the floor with her legs tucked to one side underneath her. Her eyes shut, and she cradles Perpetua's crystal in her cupped palms. Sam's as stunning as a sleeping swan, long necked, and beautiful. Seconds later, the crystal glows from within. Slowly, it lifts, hovering until it's parallel with Sam's eyes. The rock rotates haphazardly, spinning on no particular axis. Rainbows shoot from the core, projecting onto the walls, glittering like a disco ball. For a while, Sam's face never reveals anything other than serenity, and then she winces. Her face sours in pain, and she violently catapults away from the relic. It drops with a thump at the same time Sam's body smashes into the far wall.

I run to her, grabbing her face in my palms. "Sam! Wake up!" She's out cold. *What's happened?* "Sam!" I yell louder, shaking her, hoping that I can break through.

The bedroom door slams open. "What's wrong?" Turner rushes into the room, out of breath, his face red and sweaty from running. He must have been nearby, sensed my fear, and came looking for us. Gently, he gathers Sam's lifeless body into his arms and places her carefully on her bed. He inspects her with the expertise of a physician. "She'll be okay, I think. She's breathing. I'll have to run and get the nurse. What happened?" He starts to walk away.

"She was just meditating on a relic. Out of nowhere, it blew her across the room. She hit the wall pretty hard. I don't even know what happened!" I say, panicked.

"What relic?"

I run and grab it from the floor, bringing it back for Turner's inspection.

"Where did you get this?"

"It's—it's a long story."

His brow arches, but he doesn't push it. "It's a dream-drive, but not one of the Academy's. It's too large. Where did you get it?"

"Perpetua," I admit, dropping my gaze to the floor.

"So this is it. What they've been looking for, isn't it?"

Sam moans and grabs her head. We rush to the bed.

"I saw them, all of them," she says.

"Saw who?" Turner asks.

"The Underground."

No 33

MOTIVES

"THE UNDERGROUND—EVERY SINGLE MEMBER. All of their dreams are compiled onto the crystal hard drive." Sam sits up, holding both hands to her head. "It was too much information to contemplate. It blasted me out of my meditation."

"Why would the Academy want that?" I turn to Turner.

"The same reason they want to store every student's dreams, Sera," he says. "Once you know someone's hopes, dreams, and fears, you can control and manipulate them."

"So this is how they do it? How they always know the perfect thing to bribe us with?" I think of my perfect room, my perfect clothes, the perfect parties; everything was chosen, knowing that I would love it. I always knew it was too good to be true.

"So the Academy wishes to control the Underground, too?" Sam says.

"Seems so," Turner offers.

An achy sickness whirls through my stomach, giving me cramps.

"Maybe it's for good, like, to stop their attacks?" Sam stretches for optimism.

"I don't know, but the more I learn about the Society, the less likely that seems," I say. "What are we going to do? Where's Bishop? I need to talk to him."

Both fidget and refuse to meet my eyes.

"Where is he?" I demand.

"Sera, really, you shouldn't worry about it. It's late, why don't you go to bed." Turner scratches the top of his chest. Something there is missing. Something he's worn around his neck from the day he took it from me.

"Where's the rosary necklace?" I hope that he's only taken it off for the evening, but my gut tells me that's not the case. Turner laces his hands behind his head, looks to the ceiling, and blows out a sigh. "The thing is, Sera——"

"No! No! No! Please tell me you did not give the necklace to Bishop!" I've spent months preparing to meet Cece and fight her on my own. All I can think about is their last meeting, where Bishop almost died.

"I didn't," he says. "I gave it to Terease."

"You did *what?*"

"It's too late. They're gone—Bishop, Terease, and a small Society army are headed to meet Cece and the Underground."

"Why would you do that?"

"No matter the Society's intentions with the crystal, I want to see the Underground's demise as much as Bishop. I want you to be safe." He reaches out, comforting me with his warm hands. I want to be mad, but now I understand, he can't help trying to protect me, too.

"What you wanted to do with the necklace, I've known all along. I can't let you go running into danger like that. I'd kill myself if something happened to you. And for once, Bishop and I agree on something."

Turner's been protecting me from, well, me, since he realized what I had been planning all this time—going back, facing Cece, and saving my mom. I give him a weak smile.

Even with everything I've learned, what he and Bishop kept from me about Aunt Mona, how everyone's lied, I realize a small part of me doesn't blame them. I blame the Society of Wanderers. No matter what side you play for, they've manipulated us all.

"So they're on their way to Rome?"

"No. Even though they never intended to go after the Underground with the rosary relic, the Society did, last week, right after the Underground attacked the Academy. They fought with Cece and the Underground in Rome, but she got away. After that, Terease had to make new plans. Somehow, she arranged a truce meeting with them in Gibeon."

"Gibeon!" My eyes grow wide. This is my chance to finally rescue my mom. In my heart, I know she'll be there, too. I run to my room, fling open the oath package, and riffle through the contents, looking for the wandering compass.

I walk back to Sam's room with it in my hand.

"No way! I know what that is and you're not going," Turner says, pointing to the compass.

"Why? I have a whole team here." I look meaningfully at both of them.

"She knows?" Turner looks to Sam in shock.

"I do." I grab his hands and squeeze. "I know everything now. I'm sorry it's turned out this way. I'm sorry Bishop cheated you out of a team."

He blushes but relief flashes behind his eyes. Something in his demeanor changes. That hardened shell that he's always hidden behind dissolves in an instant. "I'm so sorry. I wanted to tell you for so long, but I've been forbidden." He hangs his head.

"I understand. It's not your fault. It's the Society. I'm just glad Mona did the right thing to protect both of you." I smile, even though I'm deeply hurt.

"Thank you." He kisses my hand. "That's all I ever wanted. To be recognized by you."

There's peace in this new understanding. Since I arrived, Turner's been hidden in the background, wanting nothing more than to get my attention, to be part of a team—our team. I understand him now. I push everything else that's happened in the last several hours to the back of my mind. I can deal with my emotions, my hatred for the Society later. For now I have to clear my thoughts and find my mom.

"If you don't come, I'll go without you." I hold up the wandering compass.

"I'm in." Sam stands.

Turner appears less enthused. He crosses his arms and scowls. "Fine," he relents, "but I need to get some things first. Don't move until I get back!"

Turner takes forever, but when he finally returns, he's covered in a utility suit of gadgets and weaponry. Contraptions are leather-strapped to his biceps, his thighs, and his belt, layered over a fitted black outfit.

"What the heck are you wearing?" I stifle a laugh. "You look like a steampunk tomb raider." I look him over. The outfit shows off his muscles, accentuates his broad chest and burly shoulders. I can't deny its hotness. My face flushes red. I remember our steamy kiss and look away, flustered. I have to remind myself that these are the thoughts I have no control over. My feelings for him and Bishop are artificial.

"You know you like it." He crosses his arms and flexes his biceps playfully.

"Come on, you two." Sam drags me out of the room. "The sexual tension around here is making me ill."

In the living room, we move the furniture against the walls to make way for our exit to Gibeon. Sam and I stand equidistant, each with our own wandering compass in hand. Turner has no compass, so he holds my empty hand. With synchronized precision, Sam and I each rotate our compasses in a complete circle until the speed causes a wicked buzzing sound. The living room blurs, disconnecting with true time, sending the three of us to Gibeon.

Through a confusing haze, Gibeon comes into view. The city skyline stretches three hundred and sixty degrees around us. We've entered via some kind of personal, elevated landing pad.

There are separate landing pads nearby. Wanderers from many different time periods are leaving and arriving.

The landing pad, a pedestal of sorts, descends. When it touches bottom, a staircase rotates, locking into one side. We step down and join the masses of people walking around the enormous city.

To put some kind of label on the architectural style or

the inhabitants of the city is impossible. The pedestrians, shop owners, and Society officials walking around are every color, every shape, and wearing every imaginable style of clothing. Some outfits I recognize and can easily place them in their proper time period, but others, I could have never even dreamed. A man flies in, standing on a silver disk shaped like a mini spaceship. Maybe some of these people are from the future—or another planet? At this moment, I can't be sure.

There are things that I recognize, of course. Buildings that appear ancient but are Roman, Egyptian, Chinese, Indian, or Mayan—and others that are modern. They are from every culture or time in history you can conceive. Still, in the chaos, there's an undeniable beauty in this melting pot of time, space, and culture—a utopia of compiled existence.

"This place is amazing." We can't help but stand frozen, rotating in our spots, taking in everything. Though, taking it all in is impossible. No lecture by Mr. Tash could have explained this place in mere words. Only to see its eclectic landscape is to believe it.

"I don't even know where to start." Sam gawks.

An Animate walks past and growls. The mechanical animal has the sinewy body of a lion, the head of a sphinx, and enormous wings. It yelps once before it gallops away, leaps into the opalescent sky, spreads its wings, and swoops away.

When I look to the heavens, there's a flock of similar beings flying around the city's tallest building. That building's structure is that of a ziggurat—box stacked on slightly smaller box, over and over, thousands of feet in the air. The building's silhouette creates the largest and steepest set of stairs I have ever seen. It's the Grand Hall.

Speechless, we turn and look at each other, eyes wide.

"This distracts me. I can't focus...I just want to sit here and watch everything and everyone," I say.

"I've read about it but never, ever imagined," Turner says, mouth gaping open.

"Sam, can you find Bishop in your mind?"

"They can't connect here," Turner responds.

"Why?"

"Because, there's no need for it. The same rules don't apply in Gibeon. We're here in the same time. She's going to have her own experience. She can't have her Protector's, too."

Testing the theory, Sam squeezes her eyes shut and presses her fingers to her temples, trying to see into Bishop's mind. "I've got nothing," she says, opening her eyes. "I think he's right. I should have checked in on him before we left our true time. Maybe it would have worked then."

"Any idea on how we're going to find them?" Turner asks.

I pull out my cell phone and dial Bishop. It rings several times. I'm not sure if he'll answer because he's probably still mad at me for kissing Turner. But given what he's done in the past, we should be about even.

"Sera."

"Hi, we need to chat. Where are you?"

"Yes, we do, but I'm a little busy at the moment." A clock dongs loudly in the background, drowning out his voice.

"Okay, I'll call you back later—bye!" I hang up before he has time to respond. I run to the nearest Society official I can find.

"Hi! I'm looking for the clock tower. Can you point me in the right direction?"

"Yes, it's near the Grand Lodge." He points off in the distance to the ziggurat.

"Thanks!"

I run. Turner and Sam fall into step next to me.

"How do you know where to go?" Sam asks in a pant.

"I heard the clock dong in the background of his call. It was so loud he had to be standing next to it while he was talking to me. I took a shot asking if there was one in the city."

We run about a mile before we enter the plaza with the Grand Lodge. Across the plaza stands a clock tower. The clock's face equally divides in two. On one half sits a beaming sun and on the other, a blue moon. There are no numbers. In a city with no time, there's only night and day.

I spin, looking for any sign of Terease or Bishop, but the only other living things here are the colorfully painted Animates covering every level of the Grand Lodge.

The nearest one, a woman with three eyes and several arms, wields a long sickle, which she points at me. I believe I'm about to be speared through, but then she points the sword across the way to a building behind the clock tower.

Somehow, magically, she knows who I'm looking for.

"You should make an offering," Sam suggests.

A man peddling flowers walks into the plaza. I run to him, make a quick purchase, and return to the Animate with an offering of red roses. The statue nods and returns to her original pose.

Sam, Turner, and I cross the plaza and enter the building pointed out by the Animate. The building was probably built in the late 1800s. After we enter, I immediately recognize the lush and beautiful interior as a theater.

"Let's go to the balconies," Turner says. I nod and Sam and I follow quietly as he leads us up the stairs.

From this height, no one will notice us. There are a few thousand empty seats surrounding an ornately detailed stage. We quietly duck behind seats to watch the meeting that's already taking place.

On the stage, Terease stands face-to-face with Cece. She's exactly as I remember her. Her hair, blood red, drips long over her shoulders. Her skin glows white and flawless. In her beauty, there's evil.

Society soldiers stand behind Terease, ready to attack. Likewise, Cece has brought her own guards. Exeter, her seer, and Cerberus, her Protector, move in line behind her like the vertebrae of a snake, slithering from one spot to the next.

My heart leaps at the sight of my mom. She stands behind them, next to several Underground guards. She looks different than I remember…older, much older than she did before.

She's no longer in a wheelchair—thank goodness. I can't control the excitement of seeing her again, and pop up to walk toward her. Turner grabs my sleeve and pulls me back to the floor.

"Hold on," he says. "Stay here for a few moments, and then I'll help you storm the castle." Turner takes off, running for who knows where.

Sam and I stay put, watching the exchange. Cece and Terease deliberate for quite a while. We strain to hear but can only make out limited words.

After a while, Turner returns.

"Where have you been?" I scold.

He ignores my question. "Come on, follow me." Turner takes off, back down the stairs and into the main seating area. Now we're on the same level as the stage. My mom's so close now I can hardly stand it. I just want to run to her and pull her into a hug and never let go.

Finally, Cece and Terease meet some kind of impasse, and the conversation takes an annoyed, louder tone.

"Enough of this!" Cece says in dramatic fashion. "We will abandon our attacks only if you give us the crystal!" she yells, obviously annoyed. I sit up a little straighter at the realization that the Underground attacked the Academy and my friends were hurt over the crystal I have in my pocket—the dream-drive containing the dreams of the entire Underground. *That's what they were looking for.*

"We were unable to procure the crystal ourselves, but I

have something you may personally find more interesting," Terease offers.

Cece laughs wickedly. "Terease, oh dear, Terease. I doubt there is anything you could offer in exchange for the souls of five thousand members."

Terease pulls out a crystal of her own and holds it up.

Cece sucks in a breath. She begins to reach for the crystal and then jerks her hand back delicately. "Is that what I think it is?" She stares at it in amazement.

"It is." Terease nods.

"Exeter!" Cece yells and snaps her fingers.

The bald man steps forward. He's dressed in drab monk's robes, just like the last time I saw him. The Seer only needs to point at the crystal to cause it to rise from Terease's hand. The crystal tumbles through the air, landing at an airborne spot, right above Exeter's cupped palms.

"Who do you think it belongs to?" Sam whispers.

I shrug my shoulders.

Exeter's eyes roll back into his head as he meditates on the object, searching its life path. The crystal dreamdrive burns from within, levitating in a circular motion above him. Rainbows shoot from its core, painting the walls of the theater with radiating prisms. After a few moments, the crystal falls into Exeter's grasp, and he opens his unseeing eyes.

"To whom does the dreamdrive belong?" Cece asks. She can hardly contain her excitement for whatever she hopes the answer will be.

"Seraphina Parrish," he says solemnly.

"No!" Many people scream at once. Bishop runs from a side area, where I had not originally seen him. He and my mom rush Exeter, tackling him to the floor. Both are on a path to grab my dreamdrive. An onslaught of chaos and fighting breaks out between Society soldiers and the Underground.

My minds reels, analyzing why the Underground would even accept *my* dreamdrive as an exchange—one person's dreams for five thousand people's dreams. What good would my dreamdrive do them?

Before I can put a coherent thought together, Cece spots me. She jumps from the stage, flying through the air and lands, crushing me. We crumble to the ground. I kick her off, sending her flying away. She lands on her feet, ready to attack once again.

Turner jumps in to protect me. He takes a few swipes at Cece before Cerberus, her Protector dog-beast, appears beside her. The animal's mouth foams and his fanged teeth snap. He launches his pulsing muscles at Turner. They roll away, clenched together in their own vicious fight.

Cece and I circle each other, keeping an even distance.

"I've been waiting for this for a long time," I say.

She laughs. "You forget, we know you better than you know yourself. And when you hand over the Underground's dreamdrive, we'll have everything we need. We know you have it."

I try not to appear shocked that she knows that I have the

crystal. I have no idea how she does, but she'll never get it back. I'll die first.

"Even after all this time, the Academy keeps so much from you." She smirks behind her blood red lips. "You're no better off than the last time we met you," she sneers.

"Oh, I'm better—much better." I've been waiting for this moment. I breathe deeply and smile. Then I attack.

No
35

A TRUCE

OUR COLLISION COMES IN AN EXHIBITION OF power. Cece and I are so evenly matched, it's as though she can foresee my strikes and I hers. Flip. Kick. Jab. Punch. Roll. I direct a blow to her head and change my mind at the last minute. Instead, I kick her legs out from under her. The new "change-my-mind-at-the-last-minute approach" helps. I gain the upper hand until Cece, I think, applies the same tactic.

Her knuckles crash across my jaw then again across my face. My nose instantly burns with blood. It drips uncontrollably down my lip and over my chin. At the sight, Cece's hungry eyes look as though they want to devour me. Not me, my blood. She rushes me again. I elbow her ribs, sending her crashing away.

Ricocheting, Cece leaps, soaring over my head, reaching to grab me from behind. I flip her over, throwing her body to the ground and drop both my knees onto her chest. Her ribs break and crush. At the exact same moment, Exeter and Cerberus, who have been fighting their own vicious battles, collapse in my peripheral view.

I pause for a split second at what has happened. Cece, Exeter, and Cerberus—they're connected, truly connected. To hurt one is to hurt all of them. To *kill* one may *kill* them all. I stare down at Cece, thinking I'll find her in pain, near death with punctured lungs. Instead, her mouth gapes open, and she's catching the blood dripping from my nose—sucking it like some kind of sick, messed-up vampire.

I jump back in horror.

She licks her lips and smiles. Her chest, which was caved flat, reconstructs before my eyes, expanding like a balloon. She and her team jump to their feet, apparently stronger than they were before. The fighting mayhem continues.

"Figure it out yet, Sera?" Cece paces. Some of my blood has dripped across her face. She reaches her hand to her cheek and smears it into her skin, just like she did on our first meeting. A long, deep cut on her cheek shimmers, magically returning to glowing perfection.

My blood heals her, heals all three of them.

"If you could only find my weakness, you could win this."
She laughs.

I jolt at her words. She really does know me. It's the tactic
I apply for all my fights, often helping me win.

"But you won't find any. I have none." She lures me to
the stage. "But you do. Many of them." She looks around. I
follow her eyes. Bishop fights Exeter for the crystal. Turner
struggles with the dog-beast. Together, Sam and Mom scuffle
with two Underground members. They're all fighting for me,
suffering, taking beatings, to make sure my dreamdrive does
not fall into Cece's hands.

Turner, closest to me, crashes to the ground with Cerberus growling and snapping on his chest. From his hand,
a square object skids across the floor, landing at my feet. I
look down. It's a remote. I look up and smile at Cece. "Seems
your weakness at the moment is lack of help," I say. I step on
the biggest button on the remote, knowing exactly what it's
for—holograms.

Within seconds, Cece's guards have no chance. A hundred
holographic soldiers glimmer and zap into being. Turner has
installed hologram machines around the theater. That's why
he left Sam and me earlier.

The holograms are every single beast I ever fought in the
training room and many more that I have never seen. They're
horrifying. Warriors made with a mishmash of mythological
animals, men, and women. Each carries their own weapon:
swords, knives, clubs with spikes, and other menacing tools

of violence. I always viewed the touchable holograms as training exercises, but never imagined that they could be used for true warfare.

Cece screams and leaps away. She lands on my mom, wrapping her white hand around her neck. "I'll kill her if you don't do everything I ask," she screams.

I lock eyes with my mom. Despite her situation, she smiles as though she's looking at me for the first time. She searches my eyes, as if memorizing my face, and says softly, "I've been with you always." There's a long second where I search her violet eyes, realizing that I've never heard her voice before. It's beautiful, like angelic bells and soothing wind chimes.

I'm rocked out of my thought when the floor violently shakes. An earthquake jolts, whipping us. I heave right and left while the world tilts, teetering back and forth. I fall backward onto a theater chair and grasp its armrest. Gibeon is apparently moving to a new location in time, just like Mr. Tash explained.

The theater rips apart, right down the middle. A gash opens, a crack in the earth so deep that I can't see its bottom, zigzagging the length of the main aisle of seating. The chair I've latched on to sinks, disappearing into the hole. I wobble backward with unsure footing and almost fall in. I clasp on to a nearby incline of stairs. Throwing my leg over the risers, I pull my body upward, and latch on to the edges. When I steady myself, I make my way back onto the stage.

"Whatever you want, I'll give it to you," I say to Cece as

I pull myself to my feet. My hands are held high, surrendering. I'll do anything to save my mom.

Plaster crumbles from the ceiling. Chandeliers rattle and shatter, crashing to the floor. Fighting between the Underground and the Society holograms continue despite the earthquake.

When I'm a few feet away from Cece, so close she can reach out and exchange Mom's position for my own, Cece makes a quick motion with her hands, snapping my mother's neck.

"No!" In slow motion, I reach for my mom. Her eyes shut at the moment her body hits the floor. Cece leaps over her body, ready to attack me in my most vulnerable state. She barely grasps my shoulders when Turner crashes into her, rolling her away.

I turn to see them struggle, ripping, punching, and kicking like madmen. Except they keep rolling together in their combat, moving farther away with each new strike. And finally, before I can stop it, before I can yell out, Turner and Cece whirl together over the edge of the crack created by the earthquake, plunging into the endless pit.

On hands and knees, I scurry to the edge, looking over in disbelief. My hand reaches out for Turner, ready to pull him back from death, but they're already gone, swallowed by the sinking blackness.

Gut-wrenching screams tear from my throat.

Turner—Mom—Mom—Turner. Gone. They're both gone.

I push away from the edge on all fours, then turn, collapsing onto my mother's lifeless body, like she's some kind of lifeboat that can save me from my grief. Tears, so many tears drop onto her, willing her to live.

In a moment of desperation, I grab a nearby shard of glass and puncture my palm. A steady stream of warm blood oozes from the wound, and I rub the liquid around her broken neck and let it drip into her open mouth. Cece and her team healed with my blood, so I pray that, somehow, my mom will, too.

I wait and gather her into my lap, holding her close, praying for a miracle. Minutes pass. My gaze roams her body for any indication of life, but she doesn't recover. I frantically try again but nothing happens. She's gone. Really gone. In shock, I blankly stare at her face and then off toward the pit.

Mom's gone. Turner's gone.

My screams, piercing and tormenting, give vent to my anguish, as everything that's ever been good in my soul begins to die a sickening, bitter death. I rock my mom in my arms until the earth stops shaking.

Then, for several moments, there is complete silence and stillness. I look around, taking in the eerie destruction. Amazingly, though I don't understand how, objects begin to move with the tiniest tremble again, but this time, on their own.

Life reverses in slow motion. This is real slow motion, happening in real life, not just in my head. Plaster that had fallen from the ceiling floats upward. Shards of glass rain in reverse, returning to their chandeliers. Chairs move, forcing themselves upright. Everything that's broken mends, healing to its original state of perfection.

Leaning into my mother, I rush to inspect her for any sign of life: a breath, a jolt, or any minuscule movement to give me hope. I pinch her wrist, testing for a flutter of a pulse. But still, there is none. The reversal does not affect her.

I slump back and stare at the pit, desperately hoping for Turner and Cece to reappear, emerging from the hole, returning to me. But instead, the gash closes. The fissure sews itself shut, as though it's devoured Cece and Turner, together, forever.

I SCREAM REPEATEDLY, CLUTCHING MY MOM'S body. Sam rushes to my side and pulls me into an embrace. Tears spill down her face as she tries to console me. Bishop barrels to where the pit closed, throws himself to the ground and screams, slamming the ground with his fists, willing the earth to split back open, so he can jump in to save Turner. But there's nothing he can do.

Shocked, I look around.

The fighting has stopped. The Underground, the ones who survived the chaos, have fled. Holographic soldiers, sensing the end of the fight, dematerialize, swirling into the air, leaving in electrified sparkles. Exeter and Cerberus are no-where to be found. But if Cece is dead, so are they, I suspect.

"Bishop, Sam, leave us. I must speak with Sera before more Society officials arrive," Terease says. Unfortunately, she's sur-vived. Sam and Bishop step away, but not too far. I'm sure they trust her less than before.

"Your mother." Terease looks down at my mom, still cra-dled in my arms. She tenderly sweeps a strand of dark hair away from my mother's beautiful face. "She was a great woman, ex-tremely brave," Terease says, and gently rearranges her lifeless hands, folding them on her chest.

"You knew her? You knew she was alive?" I lean down and kiss her forehead.

"Yes, I've known her since we were teenagers at the Acad-emy. She's been fighting her own war for a very long time, and now she's at peace."

"What does that even mean? What war?" I look up. There are so many things I need to ask her.

"We all have our own parts to play," Terease says, confus-ing me further. "Here," she continues, "this is your dreamdrive. Keep it and the other one close." She tucks it into my hand. "Tell the Society that both dropped into the pit with Cece. Do you understand?"

I nod, though I don't understand why I need to lie.

Society soldiers thunder into the theater. Terease and I look up. Phineas Levi, the Grand Master of the Society, storms in behind them and points to Terease.

"Arrest that woman for crimes committed against the Society," he screams.

I look at her in shock.

Terease whispers in my ear, "All you need to know is that your mom loved you. For now, whatever you do, deny that you know who she is, or you will have the same fate as me."

Two men in uniform seize her by the arms, dragging her away. But for once, she's looking at me smiling, like she knows something I don't. She doesn't engage my mind with her flame-searing eyes the way she has in the past. She looks serene. And for the first time ever, the sickly blackness that has always followed her disappears.

Sam places her hand on my shoulder. I roll my mom gently away, placing her completely on the floor, and stand.

I hide my dreamdrive in my pocket next to the Underground's.

Grand Master Levi descends. He's tall, dark-skinned, well dressed, and there's an air of dangerous authority that follows him. "Explain yourselves," he says, crossing his arms.

Bishop steps forward. "Terease Ivanov tried to offer Seraphina's dreamdrive to Cece to stop the Underground's attacks." He gestures toward me.

"Why?" He walks around, surveying the mess in the theater.

"I don't know, sir." Bishop shrugs.

"Do you have this dreamdrive?" He stops, regarding me with curiosity.

"No, sir." I step forward before Bishop can speak. "It was taken by Cece along with the Underground's dreamdrive," I lie through my tears.

"And where is Cece now?" He looks around with his hands held out.

"Dead, Grand Master. My brother, Turner, gave his life, killing her."

The Grand Master allows the information to settle. He paces, tapping his finger to his lips. Abruptly, he stops and responds, "Good."

We stiffen at the piercing word. How can a boy's death be good? A tear slips down my cheek. Sam stifles a sob.

"He's a hero. He'll receive a hero's funeral."

The Grand Master walks away momentarily, leaving us in the care of a soldier. Soon afterward, we're interrogated for hours, recounting the events repeatedly before a committee of high-ranking Society members. Several times I catch Grand Master Levi scrutinizing me with calculating eyes. His intensity makes me nervous, but thankfully, he never returns to question me himself. My intuition tells me we'll talk, eventually.

·

Two soldiers cover my mom with a sheet and lift her body, taking her away. I want to reach for her, but I have to remind myself that she's not really there, and I need to let go.

A WEEK LATER

No.
37
A Sacrifice

THE SUNSET IS PINK, PURPLE, AND CYAN BLUE. A thousand people stand at the edge of the sacred river that cuts the city of Gibeon in half. I tightly grip two white lanterns. One is for my mom and one is for Turner.

A Grand Lodge Master officiates at the ceremony, which I can barely make out through my pain. I only know that it's time to release my lanterns upon the water's surface when everyone around me bends down to do so.

My fingers dip into the cool river. The two lanterns float, bobbing. I give them a gentle push, and they drift away. This is a Wanderers' funeral. Each flickering flame symbolizes setting the deceased's soul free.

My extra lantern is the only tribute here to my mom. All the others are for Turner. To most, she's been dead for a very long time. I replay her final words repeatedly in my head. "I've been with you always." It's a sentiment that I don't completely understand. Her words are infused with a mother's love. Love that I have only seen by her actions to protect my dreamdrive from Cece.

Farther away, Mona leans in and places a lantern on the river. She sadly looks up at me from her crouched position, and I look away, still bitter for what I've learned. With the death of Turner and my mom, my emotions are compounded, perhaps even more elevated from where they were originally. Yes, I understand Mona's actions, pretending to be my aunt to protect her boys, but I'm still hurt by the deceit. Bishop appears at her side, pulling her into a hug. He glances at me, and I turn to look away.

Thousands of lanterns drift out to the center of the river, and suddenly they lift from the water's surface, slowly launching, drifting through the air. Lanterns are everywhere, dotting the sky like fireflies.

When this happens, this signals the end of the ceremony. The crowd disperses, silently walking away. But I can't force my eyes from the beauty, and perhaps, I'm not ready to let either of them go.

Alone, I walk the muddy embankment. When I reach a bridge, I climb onto a cold marble slab and tuck myself into a nook. Hidden, I watch the lanterns float above the city for hours, until I can no longer sort out the lanterns from the twinkling stars.

In a fog of sadness and confusion, I stumble off my hiding spot. There are many people walking through Gibeon, but I've never felt so alone or so dead inside. Sam and Macey are the only ones I've truly spoken with since Mom and Turner's deaths. And even that's very little. I can't make my mouth form any words that don't sound hateful. So I keep quiet, allowing angry thoughts to scream through my head. They're a turbulent mess that needs to be dealt with, but not yet. For now, I need to feel the animosity to understand the pain.

Yes, I've dreamed of going back to save both Mom and Turner. But for once, this can't be done. To die in Gibeon is final.

On several occasions, Bishop tries to explain himself. But I can't deal with him—not yet. Looking into his eyes will not calm my rage. His explanations will only ignite the fire. I hate what the Society has brought to my life: the revolting lies, the chaos, the lost choices, and the tormenting pain. I long to be Normal and to have never known this world.

•

The next morning, I'm sitting on the couch in my apartment. I've stayed awake all night. After hours of infomercials, Gabe's morning show begins. He's taking the newscast very seriously, as he reports on Cece's death, Turner's heroism, and the lingering threats of the Underground.

The next headline story discusses Terease. She's been given a hasty trial by the Grand Master Elders for infractions upon the Society, including attempting to trade my dream-drive to the Underground. The reason Cece would want it is still a mystery to me and everyone else who's tried to decipher the meaning. Clearly, Terease knows much more than others of this and certainly more about my mom. I find myself thinking of Terease's motives, often wondering what they mean, and if there's a way to seek her out to get the answers.

In the end, Terease is found guilty. She's immediately exiled to Nocturna—the wandering city for criminals where time speeds up, pressing rapid aging upon all inhabitants. Living within its walls is a death sentence.

The last story talks of Perpetua and her team, who are expelled for good, their records still marred by their previous dealings with the Underground. Maybe they just went home to their families to be Normal? Gabe doesn't say. From my perspective, the true torture would be forcing them to take the oaths to the Society.

Bishop walks into the living room, fresh from his shower. He nods, not bothering to say anything. He knows I'm not ready to talk. I wearily glance at his eyes and stand to make my way to the place I've gone every morning since Turner's death—his apartment.

The first morning I entered Turner's apartment, I barely made it past the couch. Every morning since, I've returned, acclimating myself to the heartbreaking emptiness. But then I remind myself that the apartment was always empty and lonely, just like Turner. I frown.

I stand in front of his bedroom door for several moments before I'm brave enough to walk in. When I do, the musty and stagnant air sours my stomach. Gadgets, inventions, and rolls of drawings sit on every surface. I smile at the thought of him working on them, tinkering with the inventions, bringing the machines to life. I walk along the walls, lightly touching items as I pass, wishing the relics would send me their memories of Turner, just as if I were a Seer.

Given the opportunity to look into his eyes now, I would not look away and pretend that there was no connection between us. I would live there forever, knowing he could be taken away in an instant. Those feelings, the unwanted love I feel for him, although tampered with, were ones I denied myself for months. Now, they feel raw and unresolved. Maybe he was meant to be my Protector all along. In the end, after all, isn't that what he died doing?

A stack of envelopes, shiny and silver gray, the exact color of Turner's eyes, stops me in my tracks. They sit on his desk. A pair of scissors sits next to them—and beneath those, a photo—a photo that's been cut in half.

I slide the photo out and stare at it. In the photo stands Turner, dressed up and smiling with his arm slung over someone who was next to him—before the two were separated. I pick up the photo, holding it to my eyes and feel the ragged edge. The other half of the missing photo, I realize, was of Bishop.

My emotions hitch in my chest, and my heart tightens with convulsions. I cry, so hard my stomach feels as though it will turn inside out.

"Sera," Bishop says. His hand rests lightly upon my shoulder. He's followed me.

"He—he knew he was going to die to protect me." I heave uncontrollably and turn to Bishop.

"What are you talking about?"

"Here." I hold out the envelope and the half picture. "I received a letter in the mail before I ever came to Chicago. It was in an envelope just like this, and it had *your* photo in it. After Sam told me what you did to make sure you were the Protector chosen for our team, I assumed it was you who sent the photo—so you could secure your place. But now I see, it wasn't you. It was Turner. He sent me your photo, wanting to secure your spot because he knew he'd risk his life to protect me."

My tears fall, understanding Turner's complete and utter selflessness. All of his actions from the beginning, no matter how annoying, were for me—all of them—for me.

Bishop gathers me into his arms and holds me tight.

He cries too, holding nothing back.

After a while, once our tears have slowed, I step away and hold the envelope. "He must have sent the envelope from Gibeon before we found your meeting place with Cece. The post office there can send mail to any time period." I gasp a sob.

"Yes, I'm afraid it does." He takes the envelope and photo and sets them on the desk, and then he grabs my hands.

"I'm so sorry for everything I did, Sera. I'm so, so sorry." He leans in to level his eyes with mine.

"Stop. Just stop," I say and look away. His timing couldn't be worse.

"Please, if I don't tell you now, you may never hear my side of the story."

I shake my head, staring at the floor, wiping my nose with my sleeve. *Let him say what he needs to say. Just get it over with.* "Fine," I relent.

"When I first went to the L train station, the day you arrived in Chicago, I only went to watch you from afar. I had to know who you were because I was so certain you would never choose me over Turner. Even now, I'm certain it would have never been me. I've seen the way you look at Turner through Sam's mind. The way you two kis—" He stops and stiffens before he can finish the word. He looks at the floor, composing his thoughts.

As he does, the memory of the one all-consuming kiss I shared with Turner flashes in my mind. Sadly, I have nothing to respond. I don't know whom I would have picked given the choice. Even now, I'm unsure.

"Then the Underground's gang came after you, and I had to stop them. You were in danger, and I didn't stop to consider the consequences. The instant I grabbed your arm to help you, it was done. You were mine, and I was yours. I loved you from the first moment I touched you, and I couldn't stay away from you after that. So I watched you in the court-yard of the Normals' Academy, talked to you, helped you figure out you were a Wanderer, and did many, many things I should not have. I'm so sorry for what I did to you and to Turner. I've been living with my guilt for so long, quietly making it up to you in every way I can by trying to be the perfect boyfriend. The truth is that I'm not perfect. In fact, being with you is the most selfish thing I've ever done.

"Do you think you could ever forgive me, Sera?" Bishop pleads.

I seek his eyes. I'd been uncertain what my answer would be when I thought of this moment. But I instantly know the answer. "Yes." I say it out loud, surprising myself. "We've both had our secrets. So I suppose there are things you must forgive me for, too."

"Thank you. Thank you." He moves forward for an em-brace. "My Seraphina," he whispers in my ear and leans in to kiss me.

"No!" I hold him away, acting the way I know I should, against what my body, my mind, and my heart tell me to do: to reach out and embrace him, and never let him go. There's shock and instant hurt in his red-rimmed eyes.

"Why? I love you," he says, reassuring me.

"But what we feel is still fabricated by our heritage."

"Does it matter?"

"It matters to me." I shove him away and stomp across the floor. "True, I love you. Even now, I still can't deny it." For what he's done, I shouldn't love him, and it makes me angry. "Somehow, it's irrefutable, perfectly clear. But I'm so confused by everything that's happened. I haven't figured out what to do about it. The Society is lawless, controlling our hearts, our minds, our dreams, and our souls. Do you really want to live this way—with no choice?" I swivel to face him.

"No, but this is who we are. What can we do?"

"I'm not sure yet, but I think I know someone who can help me understand everything."

"Who?"

I look down, clenching my hands into fists as I take a deep breath, considering. He won't like what I have to say, and will be even more unhappy with my daring plans. With a huff, I let my breath out in a rush, and look Bishop squarely in the eye.

"Terease."

To Be Continued

If you enjoyed this story, please take a
moment to write a review on Amazon,
Barnes & Noble, or Goodreads. By sharing
your feelings in a review, on your blog, on
Twitter, or with a friend about the book,
you support this independent author.

Special thanks to:

Tabitha Preast, Jenn Sterling, Christa Howell,
Nikki Shah, Amy Bettwy, and Deena Graves.
Beta Readers make everything better! Thank you!

Pam Berehulke,
you're still the bomb.